In praise of the *Bounty* nov
Charles Nordhoff and Jame .... Hall

Mutiny on the Bounty

"*Mutiny on the Bounty* contains the stuff of a dozen adventure novels. It is no less exciting because of its historical accuracy. The writing is remarkable in its fidelity to eighteenth-century flavor and refreshing in its charm and beauty."   — *New York Times*

"Not merely a tale of the sea; a tale of life itself, of the varying aspects of good and bad in humanity."
                        — E. F. Edgett, *Boston Transcript*

Men Against the Sea

"Seldom has a historical skeleton been so admirably tricked out in flesh and sinew. . . . You participate not merely in the excitement of casual adventure, but in the mortal triumph of this solidarity, this common stand in the face of such intensely personal terrors as hunger and thirst and loss of mind."
                        — Otis C. Ferguson, *New Republic*

"Told with the same zest and passion for veracity that distinguished *Mutiny on the Bounty*."   — William McFee, *Yale Review*

Pitcairn's Island

"A three-dimensional human story of great depth and terror and beauty."   — Archie Binns, *Saturday Review of Literature*

"One of the modern classics of the sea."
                        — Lewis Gannett, *New York Herald Tribune*

MEN AGAINST THE SEA

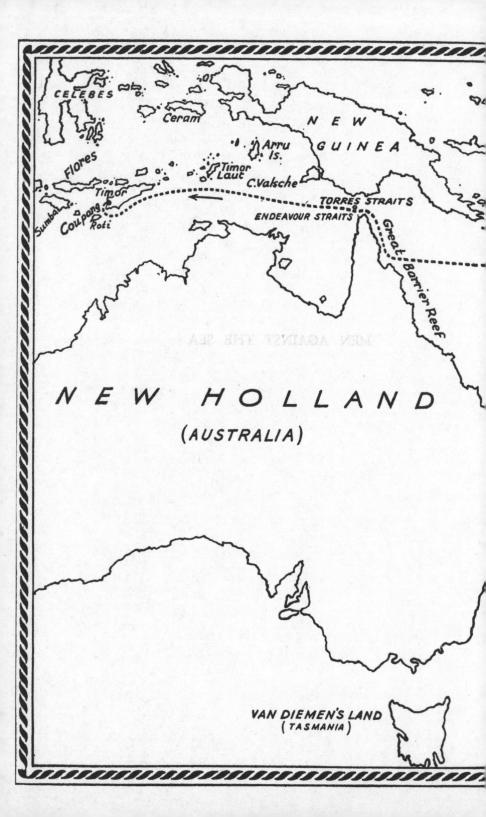

SOLOMON
ISLANDS

de Is.

NEW HEBRIDES

FEEJEE ISLANDS

Tofoa
Friendly Islands

NEW CALEDONIA

NEW ZEALAND

Books by Charles Nordhoff

The Fledgling, 1919
The Pearl Lagoon, 1924
Picaro, 1924
The Derelict, 1928

Books by James Norman Hall

Kitchener's Mob, 1916
High Adventure, 1918
On the Stream of Travel, 1926
Mid-Pacific, 1928
Mother Goose Land, 1930
Flying with Chaucer, 1930
Tale of a Shipwreck, 1934
The Friends, 1939
Doctor Dogbody's Leg, 1940
O, Millersville!, 1940
Under a Thatched Roof, 1942
Lost Island, 1944
A Word for His Sponsor, 1949
The Far Lands, 1950
The Forgotten One and Other True Tales of the South Seas, 1952
My Island Home, 1952

Books by Charles Nordhoff and James Norman Hall

History of the Lafayette Flying Corps, 1920
Faery Lands of the South Seas, 1921
Falcons of France, 1929
Mutiny on the Bounty, 1932
Men Against the Sea, 1934
Pitcairn's Island, 1934
The Hurricane, 1936
The Dark River, 1938
No More Gas, 1940
Botany Bay, 1941
Men Without Country, 1942
The High Barbaree, 1945

MEN AGAINST THE SEA

By

CHARLES NORDHOFF
and
JAMES NORMAN HALL

LITTLE, BROWN AND COMPANY
Boston   New York   London

Originally published in hardcover by Little, Brown and Company, January 1934
Reissued in paperback by Back Bay Books, July 2003

ISBN 0-316-73888-3

The Back Bay Books name and logo are trademarks of Little, Brown and Company.

Printed in the United States of America

To the memory of

CAPTAIN JOSIAH MITCHELL

of the Clipper Ship "Hornet"

who, in the year 1866, after his vessel had been lost **by**
fire, in Lat. 2° N., 110° 10′ W., safely carried fourteen
of his men, in a small open boat, to the Hawaiian Islands,
a distance of 4000 miles, after a passage of
43 days and 8 hours

FOREWORD

THE wind and weather of this narrative are those of Captain Bligh's own log. The events are those which he himself recorded so briefly there. It is hoped that the reader may, to some extent, share in the perils and hardships endured, and come to know the people of the *Bounty's* launch — who, under superb leadership, accomplished the most remarkable open-boat voyage recorded in the annals of the sea.

J. N. H.

C. N.

MEN AGAINST THE SEA

THE COMPANY OF THE BOUNTY'S LAUNCH

Lieutenant William Bligh, *Captain*
John Fryer, *Master*
Thomas Ledward, *Acting Surgeon*
David Nelson, *Botanist*
William Peckover, *Gunner*
William Cole, *Boatswain*
William Elphinstone, *Master's Mate*
William Purcell, *Carpenter*

Thomas Hayward
John Hallet   } *Midshipmen*
Robert Tinkler

John Norton
Peter Lenkletter } *Quartermasters*

George Simpson, *Quartermaster's Mate*
Lawrence Lebogue, *Sailmaker*
Mr. Samuel, *Clerk*
Robert Lamb, *Butcher*

John Smith
Thomas Hall } *Cooks*

CHAPTER I

THIS day my good friend William Elphinstone was
laid to rest, in the Lutheran churchyard on the east
bank of the river, not five cable-lengths from the
hospital. Mr. Sparling, Surgeon-General of Batavia,
helped me into the boat, and two of his Malay servants were waiting on the bank, with a litter to convey me to the grave.

Two others of our little company, worn out by the
hardships of the voyage, and easy victims to the climate of Java, have preceded Elphinstone to the
churchyard. They were men of humble birth, but
Elphinstone should be well content to lie beside them,
for they were Englishmen worthy of the name.
Lenkletter was one of the *Bounty*'s quartermasters,
and Hall a cook. Mr. Sparling had dosed them with
bark and wine, doing everything in his power to save
their lives; but they had been through too much. Mr.
Fryer, the master, Cole, the boatswain, and two midshipmen, Hayward and Tinkler, were rowed four
miles up the river to attend the funeral.

After we had paid our last respects to the master's
mate, I was grieved to learn that my friends had been

informed by the Sabandar that they were to sail for
Europe on the morrow, with the last of the *Bounty's*
people, aboard the *Hollandia,* a ship of the Dutch
East India Company's fleet. Grieved for myself, I
must add, but glad for the sake of the others, whose
longing for England, after an absence of nearly two
years, was as great as my own. The deep ulcer on my
leg, aggravated by the tropical climate, renders it
imprudent to take passage at this time; in Mr. Sparling's opinion I shall be unable to travel for several
months. I am grateful for the friendship of my
Dutch colleague and sensible of the deep obligations
he has placed me under, yet I am taking up my pen
to ward off the sense of loneliness already descending
upon me in this far-off place.

The seaman's hospital is a model of its kind: large,
commodious, airy, and judiciously divided into wards,
each one a separate dwelling in which the sick are
accommodated according to their complaints. I am
lodged with the Surgeon-General, in his house at the
extremity of one wing; he has had a cot placed for me,
on a portion of his piazza shaded by flowering shrubs
and vines, where I may pass the hours of the day
propped up on pillows — to read or write, if I choose,
or to sit in idleness with my bandaged leg extended
upon a chair, gazing out on the rich and varied land-
scape, steaming in the heat of the sun. But now
that my shipmates will no longer be able to visit me,
the hours will drag sadly. My host is the kindest of

men, and the only person here with whom I can converse, but the performance of his duties leaves little time for idle talk. His lady, a young and handsome niece of M. Vander Graaf, the Governor of Cape Town, has been more than kind to me. She is scarcely twenty, and the Malay costumes she wears become her mightily: silk brocade and jewels, and her thick flaxen hair dressed high on her head and pinned with a comb of inlaid tortoise shell. Escorted by her Malay girls, she often comes of an afternoon to sit with me. Her blue eyes express interest and compassion as she glances at me and turns to speak with her servants, in the Malay tongue. I have been so long without the pleasure of female company that it is a satisfaction merely to look at Mme. Sparling; were I able to converse with her, the hours would be short indeed.

When we had buried Mr. Elphinstone, and I had asked the Surgeon-General for writing materials, it was his wife who brought me what I required. She took leave of me soon after; and since night is still distant, I am beginning to set my memories in order for the task with which I hope to while the hours away until I am again able to walk.

Of the mutiny on board His Majesty's armed transport *Bounty*, I shall have little to say. Captain Bligh has already written an account of how the ship was seized; and Mr. Timotheus Wanjon, secretary to the governor at Coupang, has translated it into the Dutch language so that the authorities in these parts may be

on the lookout for the *Bounty* in the unlikely event
that she should be steered this way. He questioned
each of us fully as to what we had seen and heard
on the morning of the mutiny; I should be guilty of
presumption were I to set down an independent narrative based upon my own knowledge of what occurred. But of our subsequent adventures in the
ship's launch I feel free to write, the more so since
Mr. Nelson, the botanist, who informed me at Coupang that he meditated the same task, died in Timor,
the first victim of the privations we had undergone.

Never, perhaps, in the history of the sea has a captain performed a feat more remarkable than Mr.
Bligh's, in navigating a small, open, and unarmed boat
— but twenty-three feet long, and so heavily laden
that she was in constant danger of foundering — from
the Friendly Islands to Timor, a distance of three
thousand, six hundred miles, through groups of
islands inhabited by ferocious savages, and across a
vast uncharted ocean. Eighteen of us were huddled
on the thwarts as we ran for forty-one days before
strong easterly gales, bailing almost continually to
keep afloat, and exposed to torrential rains by day
and by night. Yet, save for John Norton, — murdered by the savages at Tofoa, — we reached Timor
without the loss of a man. For the preservation of
our lives we have Captain Bligh to thank, and him
alone. We reached the Dutch East Indies, not by
a miracle, but owing to the leadership of an officer of

indomitable will, skilled in seamanship, stern to preserve discipline, cool and cheerful in the face of
danger. His name will be revered by those who accompanied him for as long as they may live.

On the morning of April 28, 1789, the *Bounty* was
running before a light easterly breeze, within view
of the island of Tofoa, in the Friendly Archipelago.
I was awakened a little after daybreak by Charles
Churchill, the master-at-arms, and John Mills, the
gunner's mate, who informed me that the ship had
been seized by Fletcher Christian, the acting lieutenant, and the greater part of the ship's company,
and that I was to go on deck at once. These men
were of Christian's party. Churchill was armed with
a brace of pistols, and Mills with a musket. I dressed
in great haste and was then marched to the upper
deck. It will be understood with what amazement
and incredulity I looked about me. To be aroused
from a quiet sleep to find the ship filled with armed
men, and Captain Bligh a prisoner in their midst, so
shocked and stupefied me that, at first, I could
scarcely accept the evidence of my eyes.

There was nothing to be done. The mutineers
were in complete possession of the ship, and those
who they knew would remain loyal to their commander were so carefully guarded as to preclude all
possibility of resistance. I was ordered to stand by
the mainmast with William Elphinstone, master's

mate, and John Norton, one of the quartermasters. Two of the seamen, armed with muskets, the bayonets fixed, were stationed over us; and I well remember one of them, John Williams, saying to me: "Stand ye there, Mr. Ledward. We mean ye no harm, but, by God, we'll run ye through the guts if ye make a move toward Captain Bligh!"

Elphinstone, Norton, and I tried to recall these men to their senses; but their minds were so inflamed by hatred toward Captain Bligh that nothing we could say made the least impression upon them. He showed great resolution; and, although they threatened him repeatedly, he outfaced the ruffians and dared them to do their worst.

I had been standing by the mainmast only a short time when Christian, who had been chief of those guarding Mr. Bligh, gave this business into the charge of Churchill and four or five others, that he might hasten the work of sending the loyal men out of the ship. It was only then that we learned what his plans were, and we had no time to reflect upon the awful consequences to us of his cruelty and folly. The ship was in an uproar, and it was a near thing that Bligh was not murdered where he stood. It had been the plan of the mutineers to set us adrift in the small cutter; but her bottom was so rotten that they were at last persuaded to let us have the launch, and men were now set to work clearing her that she might be swung over the side. Whilst this was being done,

I caught Christian's eye, and he came forward to where I stood.

"Mr. Ledward, you may stay with the ship if you choose," he said.

"I shall follow Captain Bligh," I replied.

"Then into the launch with you at once," he said.

"Surely, Mr. Christian," I said, "you will not send us off without medical supplies, and I must have some cloathes for myself."

He called to Matthew Quintal, one of the seamen: "Quintal, take Mr. Ledward to his cabin, and let him have what cloathing he needs. He is to take the small medicine chest, but see to it that he takes nothing from the large one."

He then left me abruptly, and that was my last word with this misguided man who had doomed nineteen others to hardships and sufferings beyond the power of the imagination to describe.

The small medicine chest was provided with a handle, and could easily be carried by one man. Fortunately, I had always kept it fully equipped for expeditions that might be made away from the ship; it had its own supply of surgical instruments, sponges, tourniquets, dressings, and the like, and a hasty examination assured me that, in the way of medicines, it contained most of those specifics likely to be needed by men in our position. Quintal watched me narrowly while I was making this examination. I put into the chest my razors, some handkerchiefs, my only remaining packet of snuff, and half a dozen wine-glasses, which later proved of great use to us. Having gathered together some additional articles of cloathing, I was again conducted to the upper deck. The launch was already in the water; Captain Bligh, John Fryer, — the master, — the boatswain, William Cole, and many others had been sent into her. Churchill halted me at the gangway to make an examination of the medicine chest. He then ordered me into the boat, and the chest and my bundle of cloathing were handed down to me.

I was among the last to go into the launch; indeed, there were but two who followed me — Mr. Samuel, the captain's clerk, and Robert Tinkler, a midshipman. The launch was now so low in the water that Mr. Fryer, as well as Captain Bligh himself, begged that no more men should be sent into her; yet there were, I believe, two midshipmen and three or four seamen who would have come with us had there been room. Fortunately for us and for them, they were not permitted to do so, for we had no more than seven or eight inches of freeboard amidships. There were, in fact, nineteen of us in the launch, which was but twenty-three feet long, with a beam of six feet, nine inches. In depth she was, I think, two feet and nine inches. Each man had brought with him his bundle of cloathing; and with these, and the supplies of food allowed us by the mutineers, we were dangerously overladen.

But there was no time, as yet, to think of the seriousness of our situation. The launch was veered astern, and for another quarter of an hour or thereabouts we were kept in tow. The mutineers lined the *Bounty's* rail, aft, hooting and jeering at us; but it was to Mr. Bligh that most of their remarks were addressed. As I looked up at them, I found myself wondering how a mutiny into which well over half the ship's company had been drawn could have been planned without so much as a hint of danger having come to the knowledge of the rest of us. I personally had observed no sign of disaffection in the ship's company. To be sure, I had witnessed, upon more than one occasion, instances of the rigour of Captain Bligh's disciplinary measures. He is a man of violent temper, stern and unbending in the performance of what he considers to be his duty; but the same may be said of the greater part of the ships' captains in His Majesty's service. Knowing the necessity for strict discipline at sea, and the unruly nature of seamen as a class, I by no means considered that Captain Bligh's punishments exceeded in severity what the rules and necessities of the service demanded; nor had I believed that the men themselves thought so. But they now showed a passion of hatred toward him that astonished me, and reviled him in abominable language.

I heard one of them shout, "Swim home, you old bastard!" "Aye, swim or drown!" yelled another,

"God damn you, we're well rid of you!" And another: "You'll flog and starve us no more, you . . ."
Then followed a string of epithets it may be as well
to omit. However, I must do their company the
justice to say that most of the jeering and vile talk
came from four or five of the mutinous crew. I
observed that others looked down at us in silence,
and with a kind of awe—as though they had just
realized the enormity of the crime they were com-
mitting.

They had given us nothing with which to defend
ourselves amongst the savages, and urgent requests
were made for some muskets. These were met with
further abuse; but at length four cutlasses were
thrown down to us, and for all our pleading we were
given nothing else. This so enraged Captain Bligh
that he stood in his place and addressed the ruffians
as they deserved. Two or three of the seamen leveled
their pieces at him; and it was only the superior force
of his will, I believe, which prevented them from
shooting. We heard one of them cry out: "Bear off,
and give 'em a whiff of grape!" At this moment the
painter of the launch was cast off, and the ship drew
slowly away from us. I cannot believe that even
the most hardened of the mutineers was so lost to
humanity as to have turned one of the guns upon a
boatload of defenseless men, but others of our number
thought differently. The oars were at once gotten
out, and we pulled directly astern; but the ship was

kept on her course, and soon it was clear to all that
we had nothing more to fear from those aboard of
her.

At this time the *Bounty* was under courses and top-
sails; the breeze was of the lightest, and the vessel
had little more than steerageway. As she drew off,
we saw several of the men run aloft to loose the top-
gallant sails. The shouting grew fainter, and soon
was lost to hearing. In an hour's time the vessel was
a good three miles to leeward; in another hour she was
hull down on the horizon.

I well remember the silence that seemed to flow in
upon our little company directly we had been cast
adrift — the wide silence of mid-ocean, accentuated
by the faint creaking of the oars against the tholepins.
We rowed six oars in the launch, but were so deeply
laden that we made slow progress toward the island
of Tofoa, to the northeast of us and distant about
ten leagues. Fryer sat at the tiller. Captain Bligh,
Mr. Nelson, Elphinstone, — the master's mate, — and
Peckover, the gunner, were all seated in the stern
sheets. The rest of us were crowded on the thwarts
in much the same positions as those we had taken
upon coming into the launch. Bligh was half turned
in his seat, gazing sombrely after the distant vessel;
nor, during the next hour, I think, did he once re-
move his eyes from her. He appeared to have forgotten the rest of us, nor did any of us speak to re-
mind him of our presence. Our thoughts were as

gloomy as his own, and we felt as little inclined to express them.

My sympathy went out to Mr. Bligh in this hour of bitter disappointment; I could easily imagine how appalling the ruin of his plans must have appeared to him at a time when he had every expectation of completing them to the last detail. We had been homeward bound, the mission of our long voyage — that of collecting breadfruit plants in Otaheite, to be carried to the West Indies — successfully accomplished. This task, entrusted to his care by His Majesty's Government through the interest of his friend and patron, Sir Joseph Banks, had deeply gratified him, and well indeed had he justified that trust. Now, in a moment, his sanguine hopes were brought to nothing. His ship was gone; his splendid charts of coasts and islands were gone as well; and he had nothing to show for all the long months of careful and painstaking labour. He found himself cast adrift with eighteen of his company in his own ship's launch, with no more than a compass, a sextant, and his journal, in the midst of the greatest of oceans and thousands of miles from any place where he could look for help. Small wonder if, at that time, he felt the taste of dust and ashes in his mouth.

For an hour we moved slowly on toward Tofoa, the most northwesterly of the islands composing the Friendly Archipelago. This group had been so christened by Captain Cook; but our experiences among its inhabitants, only a few days before the mutiny, led us to believe that Cook must have called them "friendly" in a spirit of irony. They are a virile race, but we had found them savage and treacherous in the extreme, as different as could be imagined from the Indians of Otaheite. Only the possession of firearms had saved us from being attacked and overcome whilst we were engaged in wooding and watering on the island of Annamooka. Tofoa we had not visited, and as I gazed at the faint blue outline on the horizon I tried, with little success, to convince myself that our experiences there might be more fortunate.

Many an anxious glance was turned in Captain Bligh's direction, but for an hour at least he remained in the same position, gazing after the distant ship. When at length he turned away, it was never to look toward her again. He now took charge of his new command with an assurance, a quiet cheerfulness, that heartened us all. He first set us to work to bring some order into the boat. We were, as I have said, desperately crowded; but when we had stored away our supplies we had elbowroom at least. Our first care was, of course, to take stock of our provisions. We found that we had sixteen pieces of pork, each weighing about two pounds; three bags of bread of fifty pounds each; six quarts of rum, six bottles of wine, and twenty-eight gallons of water in three ten-gallon kegs. We also had four empty barricos, each capable of holding eight gallons. The carpenter,

Purcell, had succeeded in fetching away one of his tool chests, although the mutineers had removed many of the tools before allowing it to be handed down. Our remaining supplies, outside of personal belongings, consisted of my medicine chest, the launch's two lugsails, some spare canvas, two or three coils of rope, and a copper pot, together with some odds and ends of boat's gear which the boatswain had had the forethought to bring with him.

To show how deeply laden we were, it is enough to say that my hand, as it rested on the gunwale, was repeatedly wet with drops of water from the small waves that licked along the sides of the boat. Fortunately, the sea was calm and the sky held a promise of good weather, at least for a sufficient time to enable us to reach Tofoa.

Reliefs at the oars were changed every hour, each of us taking his turn. Gradually the blue outline of the island became more distinct, and by the middle of the afternoon we had covered well over half the distance to it. About this time the faint breeze freshened and came round to the southeast, which enabled us to get up one of our lugsails. Captain Bligh now took the tiller and we altered our course to fetch the northern side of the island. Not eighteen hours before I had had, by moonlight, what I thought was my last view of Tofoa, and Mr. Nelson and I were computing the time that would be needed, if all went well, to reach the islands of the West Indies where we were

to discharge our cargo of young breadfruit trees.
Little we dreamed of the change that was to take
place in our fortunes before another sun had set. I
now cast about in my mind, trying to anticipate what
Captain Bligh's plan for us might be. Our only hope
of succour would lie in the colonies in the Dutch
East Indies, but they were so far distant that the
prospect of reaching one of them seemed fantastic.
I thought of Otaheite, where we could be certain of
kindly treatment on the part of the Indians, but that
island was all of twelve hundred miles distant and
directly to windward. In view of these circumstances, Mr. Bligh would never attempt a return
there.

Meanwhile we proceeded on our way under a sky
whose serenity seemed to mock at the desperate plight
of the men in the tiny boat crawling beneath it.
The sun dipped into the sea behind us, and in the light
that streamed up from beyond the horizon the island
stood out in clear relief. We estimated the peak of
its central mountain to be about two thousand feet
high. It was a volcano, and a thin cloud of vapour
hung above it, taking on a saffron colour in the afterglow. We were still too far distant at sunset to have
seen the smoke of any fires of its inhabitants. Mr.
Bligh was under the impression that the place was
uninhabited. All eyes turned toward the distant
heights as darkness came on, but the only light to be
seen was the dull red glow from the volcano reflected

upon the cloud above it. When we were within a mile of the coast, the breeze died away and the oars were again gotten out. We approached the rocky shore until the thunder of the surf was loud in our ears; but in the darkness we could see no place where a landing might be made. Cliffs, varying in height from fifty to several hundred feet, appeared to fall directly to the sea; but when we had coasted a distance of several miles we discovered a less forbidding spot, where we might lie in comparative safety through the night.

There was but little surf here, and the sound of it only served to make deeper and more impressive the stillness of the night. Our voices sounded strangely distinct in this silence. For all the fact that we had not eaten since the previous evening, none of us had thought of food; and when Bligh suggested that we keep our fast until morning, there was no complaint from any of the company. He did, however, serve a ration of grog to each of us, and it was at this time that I had reason to be glad of putting the wine-glasses into my medicine chest, for we discovered that we had but one other drinking vessel, a horn cup belonging to the captain. The serving of the grog put all of us in a much more cheerful frame of mind — not, certainly, because of the spirits it contained, but rather because it was a customary procedure and served to make us forget, for the moment at least, our forlorn situation. Two men were set at the oars to

keep the boat off the rocks, and Captain Bligh commended the rest of us to take what rest our cramped
positions might afford.   The light murmur of talk
now died away; but the silence that followed was that
of tired but watchful men drawn together in spirit
by the coming of night and the sense of common
dangers.

Chapter II

THROUGHOUT the night the launch was kept close under the land. I had as my near companions Elphinstone, — the master's mate, — and Robert Tinkler, youngest of the *Bounty's* midshipmen, a lad of fifteen. The forebodings of the older part of our company were not shared by Tinkler, whose natural high spirits had thus far been kept in check by his wholesome awe of Captain Bligh. He had no true conception of our situation at this time, and it speaks well for him that when, soon enough, he came to an understanding of the dangers surrounding us, his courage did not fail him.

He had slept during the latter part of the night, curled up in the bottom of the boat with my feet and his bundle of cloathing for his pillow. Elphinstone and I had dozed in turn, leaning one against the other, but our cramped position had made anything more than a doze impossible. We were all awake before the dawn, and as soon as there was sufficient light we proceeded in a northeasterly direction along the coast. It was a forbidding-looking place, viewed from the vantage point of a small and deeply laden ship's boat. The shore was steep to, and we found no place where a landing might have been made without serious risk of wrecking the launch. Presently we were out of the lee, and found the breeze so strong and the sea so rough that we turned back to examine that part of the coast which lay beyond the spot where we had spent the night. About nine o'clock we came to a cove, and, as there appeared to be no more suitable shelter beyond, we ran in and dropped a grapnel about twenty yards from the beach.

We were on the lee side here, but this circumstance alone was in our favour. The beach was rocky, and the foreshore about the cove had a barren appearance that promised nothing to relieve our wants. It was shut in on all sides by high, rocky cliffs, and there appeared to be no means of entrance or exit save by the sea. Captain Bligh stood up in his seat, examining the place carefully whilst the rest of us awaited his decision. He turned to Mr. Nelson with a wry smile.

"By God, sir," he said, "if you can find us so much as an edible berry here, you shall have my ration of grog at supper."

"I'm afraid the venture is safe enough," Mr. Nelson replied. "Nevertheless, I shall be glad to try."

"That we shall do," said Bligh; then, turning to the master, "Mr. Fryer, you and six men shall stay with the launch." He then told off those who were to remain on board, whereupon they slackened away until we were in shallow water and the rest of us waded ashore.

The beach was composed of heaps of stones worn round and smooth by the action of the sea, and although the surf was light, the footing was difficult until we were out of the water. Robert Lamb, the butcher, turned his ankle before he had taken half a dozen steps, and thus provided me with my first task as surgeon of the *Bounty's* launch. The man had received a bad sprain that made it impossible for him to walk. He was supported to higher ground, where Captain Bligh — quite rightly, I think — gave him a severe rating. We were in no position to have helpless men to care for, and Lamb's accident was the result of a foolish attempt to run across a beach of loose stones.

The land about the cove was gravelly soil covered with coarse grass, small thickets of bush, and scattered trees. The level ground extended inland for a short distance, to the base of all but vertical walls covered with vines and fern. Near the beach we found the remains of an old fire, but we were soon convinced that the cove was used by the Indians only as a place of occasional resort.

Mr. Bligh delegated his clerk Samuel, Norton, Purcell, Lenkletter, and Lebogue as a party to attempt to scale the cliffs. Purcell carried one of the cutlasses, the others provided themselves with stout sticks. Thus armed, they set out; and were soon lost to view amongst the trees. They carried with them the copper kettle and an Indian calabash we had found hanging

from a tree near the beach. The rest of us separated,
some to search for shellfish among the rocks, others to
explore the foreshore. Nelson and I bore off to the
left side of the cove, where we discovered a narrow
valley; but we soon found our passage blocked by a
smooth wall of rock, thirty or forty feet high. Not
a drop of water could we find, and the arid aspect
of the valley as a whole showed only too plainly that
the rainfall, on this side of the island at least, must be
scant indeed.

Having explored with care that part of the cove
which Bligh had asked us to examine, we sat down
to rest for a moment. Nelson shook his head with a
faint smile.

"Mr. Bligh was safe enough in offering me his tot
of grog," he said. "We shall find nothing here, Ledward—neither food nor water."

"How do you feel about our prospects?" I asked.

"I have not allowed myself to think of them thus
far," he replied. "We can, undoubtedly, find water
on the windward side, and perhaps food enough
to maintain us for a considerable period. Beyond
that . . ." He broke off, leaving the sentence unfin-
ished. Presently he added: "Our situation is not quite
hopeless. That is as much as we can say."

"But it is precisely the kind of situation Bligh was
born to meet," I said.

"It is; I grant that; but what can he do, Ledward?
Where in God's name can we go? We know only too

well what treacherous savages these so-called 'Friendly Islanders' are; our experiences at Annamooka taught us that. I speak frankly. The others I shall try to encourage as much as possible, but there need be no play-acting between us two."

Nelson talked in a quiet, even voice which made his words all the more impressive. He was not a man to look on the dark side of things; but we had long been friends, and, as he had said, there was no need of anything but frankness between us as we canvassed the possibilities ahead.

"What I think Bligh will do," he went on, "is to take us back to Annamooka — either there or Tongataboo."

"There seems to be nothing else he can do," I replied, "unless we can establish ourselves here."

"No. And mark my words — sooner or later we shall have such a taste of Friendly Island hospitality as we may not live either to remember or regret. . . . Ledward, Ledward!" he said, with a rueful smile. "Think of our happy situation a little more than twenty-four hours back, when we were talking of home there by the larboard bulwarks! And think of my beautiful breadfruit garden, all in such a flourishing state! What do you suppose those villains will do with my young trees?"

"I've no doubt they have flung the lot overboard before this," I replied.

"I fear you are right. They jettisoned us; it is

not likely that their treatment of the plants will be any more tender. And I loved them as though they were my own children!"

We returned to the beach, where we found that the others had been no more successful than ourselves; but the exploring party had gotten out of the cove, although how they had managed it no one knew. Captain Bligh had found a cavern in the rocky wall, about one hundred and fifty paces from the beach; and the hard, foot-trampled ground within showed that it had been often used in the past. The cavern was perfectly dry; not so much as a drop of water trickled from the rocks overhead. One find we made there was not of a reassuring nature. On a shelf of rock there were ranged six human skulls which, an examination convinced me, had been those of living men not more than a year or two earlier. In one of these, the squamosal section of the temporal bone had been crushed, and another showed a jagged hole through the parietal bone. I was interested to observe the splendid teeth in each of these skulls; there was not one in an imperfect condition. These relics, gleaming faintly white in the dim light of the cave, were eloquent in their silence; and I have no doubt that they might have been more eloquent still, could they have conveyed to us information as to how they came to be there.

Shortly after midday the exploring party returned, utterly weary, their cloathing torn and their arms and legs covered with scratches and bruises. In the kettle they had about six quarts of water, and three more in the calabash. This they had found in holes amongst the rocks; but they had discovered neither stream nor spring, nor any sign of people. They had gone a distance of about two miles over rough ground where it was plain, they said, that no one had lived or could live. It was the opinion of all that the island was uninhabited. We then returned to the launch, for there appeared to be no chance of bettering ourselves here.

Again on the boat, we broke our fast for the first time since leaving the *Bounty*. Each man had a morsel of bread, a tasty bit of pork, and a glass of water. It was a short repast, and as soon as the last man had been served, we got in the grapnel and rowed out of the cove.

"We must try to get around to the windward side," said Bligh. "I fancy we shall find water there. Do you agree, Mr. Nelson?"

"It seems likely," Nelson replied. "As we were approaching yesterday, I observed that the vegetation appeared much greener to windward."

The wind was at E.S.E., and as we drew out of the shelter of the land it blew strong, with a rough, breaking sea. Close-hauled on the starboard tack, the launch heeled to the gusts, while water poured in over the lee gunwale and the people worked hard with the bails. Bluff-bowed, and deeply laden as she was, our boat buried her nose in each breaking wave, sending up great sheets of spray. Even Mr. Bligh began to look anxious.

"Stand by to come about!" he shouted, and then: "Hard alee!"

The launch headed up into the seas, while the halyards were slacked away and the gaffs passed around to the starboard sides of the masts. The sails slatted furiously as we bore off on the other tack.

Then, perceiving the danger in the nick of time, Bligh roared: "Over the side with you — those who can swim!"

It was no pleasant prospect, leaping into a sea so rough; but about half of our number sprang into the water to fend for themselves. The launch was so heavy that she answered her helm but sluggishly, and, though the foresail was backed, she was slow in bearing off. Caught directly in the trough of the sea, I am convinced that she would have foundered had we not obeyed Bligh instantly.

By the grace of God and the captain's skill, she bore off without filling. The swimmers scrambled in over the gunwales, the sails were trimmed once more, and we ran back to the shelter of the land.

We proceeded for several miles beyond the cove, and were presently rejoiced to see a clump of coconut palms standing out against the sky on the cliffs above us; but they were at such a height that we despaired of reaching them; furthermore, there was a high surf to make landing difficult. But young Tinkler and Thomas Hall were eager to make the attempt, and Bligh consented that they should try. We rowed as close to the rocks as we dared, and the two, having removed their cloathes, sprang into the sea, carrying with them each a rope that we might haul them back in case they came to grief. We might have spared ourselves the anxiety. They were as much at home in the water as the Indians themselves. We saw them disappear in a smother of foam, and when next seen, they were well out of danger and scrambling up the rocks. In less than an hour's time they returned to to the shore with about twenty coconuts, which they fastened in clusters to the line, and we then hauled them to the boat.

We rowed farther along the coast, but, toward the middle of the afternoon, having found no shelter, nor any signs of water, Captain Bligh deemed it best to return to the cove for the night. We reached our anchorage about an hour after dark. It is hardly necessary to say that every man of us was now ravenously hungry. Captain Bligh issued a coconut to each person; and the meat of the nut, together with the cool liquid it contained, proved a most welcome, but by no means a satisfying, meal.

The following morning we made our third unsuccessful attempt to get round by sea to the windward side of the island. The sky was clear, but the wind was not diminished, and we were set to bailing the moment we were out of shelter of the land. This third experience made it only too clear that we could not hope to go counter to a heavy sea in our deeply laden boat, and we were thankful indeed that we had a refuge at hand. There was nothing we could do but return to the cove.

Bligh was determined that we should keep our meagre supply of food and water intact, and although, in view of the unsuccessful expedition of the day before, we had little hope of finding anything on this side of the island, we decided to try again. Therefore, Mr. Bligh, Nelson, Elphinstone, Cole, and myself set out to examine the cliffs once more, and we were so fortunate as to discover a way to and from the cove evidently used by the Indians themselves. In a narrow gully which had escaped earlier notice, we found some large, woody vines firmly attached in clefts of the rock and to trees overhead. We could see in the walls of the cliff footholds which the Indians had constructed to assist them in making the ascent. We stood for a moment examining this crude ladder.

"Shall I try it, sir?" Elphinstone asked.

"You stand an excellent chance of breaking your neck, my lad," Bligh replied; "but if the Indians can do it, we can."

Elphinstone climbed a little way until he could reach the vines, which were of the thickness of a man's forearm. Finding that they could easily support his weight, he proceeded, while we watched him from below. After an all but vertical climb of forty or fifty feet, he reached a ledge of rock that gave him a resting place, where he turned and called down to us.

It was, in all truth, a perilous climb, particularly so for Cole, who was a heavy man and encumbered with our copper kettle, which he carried over his shoulder. A series of gigantic natural steps brought us at last to the summit, between three and four hundred feet above the sea. The latter part of the climb had been less difficult; but, for all that, we little relished the thought of a return.

From this vantage point we had an excellent view of the volcano, which appeared to rise from somewhere near the centre of the island. The intervening country was much cut up by ridges and gullies, and had an even more desolate look than when viewed from the sea. Nevertheless, we set out in the direction of the central mountain, and presently entered a deeper gully that appeared to offer a promise of water; but all that we found were a few tepid pools amongst the rocks, so shallow that it was tedious work scooping the water into the kettle with our coconut-shell ladle. We collected in all three or four gallons. Leaving our kettle here, we went on; and presently came to some abandoned huts, fallen to ruin, and near them what had once been a plantain walk, but so concealed by weeds and bushes that it was a near thing we had missed it. We got three small bunches of plantains, which we slung to a pole, for carrying in the Indian fashion. We continued inland for another mile, but the country became more and more arid, covered in places by ashes and lava beds where only a few hardy shrubs found nourishment. Evidently, we could hope for nothing more in this direction, so we returned, taking up our kettle on the way, and it was near noon before we reached the cliffs above the cove. Bligh, Nelson, and myself had each a bunch of plantains, fastened across our backs with pieces of rope. Elphinstone and Cole took charge of the kettle of water, and I still wonder that they were able to carry it down without, I believe, the loss of so much as a drop of the precious supply.

It was but natural that the thought of food should by this time be uppermost in every man's mind. Realizing the need of sustaining our strength, Captain Bligh allowed us the most substantial meal we had yet enjoyed, consisting of two boiled plantains per man, with an ounce of pork and a wineglass of water. We had combed the beach all round the cove for shellfish without finding so much as a sea snail. As it was impossible to leave the cove on account of the heavy sea, another exploring party was sent out after dinner, but they returned at sunset without having had any success. There yet remained one direction in which none of our parties had gone — toward the northwest — and the following morning near half of our party, who had spent the night in the cavern that they might have a more refreshing sleep, were sent out in a last attempt to secure food and water. Mr. Fryer was in charge of the expedition, and Captain Bligh ordered him not to return until he was convinced that we had nothing to hope for in that direction.

They were gone a full five hours, returning about ten o'clock, empty-handed, and with Robert Tinkler missing. He had become separated from the others, Fryer said, shortly before the decision to return was made. Bligh flew into a passion at this news.

"What, sir?" he roared at Fryer. "Do you mean to say that you, the ship's master, cannot keep a party of seven together? Damn your eyes! Must I go *everywhere* with you? Get you back at once and find him! Go, the lot of you, and don't come back without him!"

Silently the men set out; but they had not reached the foot of the cliffs when they heard a shout from above—and presently came Tinkler, carrying an Indian calabash containing about a gallon of water, and followed by an Indian woman and two men. The men had a cluster of husked coconuts on a pole between them.

This good fortune came at a time when it was needed, and I was glad to see that Bligh, who had been cursing the lad during his absence, forgot his anger and commended him warmly. Tinkler was pleased as only a boy can be who has succeeded in a matter in which his elders have failed. He had discovered the Indians near a hut in a small, hidden valley, and had made them understand that they were to come with him, bringing food and water.

The men were strongly made, bold-looking fellows, and appeared not at all surprised to find us there. They were unarmed, and naked except for a kirtle of tapa about the middle. The woman was a handsome wench of about twenty, and carried a child on her hip. They put down their load of coconuts and squatted near by, looking at us without the least sign of fear.

After our long sojourn at Otaheite, a good many of us had a fair knowledge of the Indian language as spoken there. We had already found that the speech of the natives of Annamooka, although allied to that of the Otaheitians, differed greatly from it; nevertheless, we could, after a fashion, converse with these people. Mr. Nelson was the best linguist amongst us, and he now questioned the men, asking first about the number of inhabitants on the island and the possibility of procuring food and water. One of them replied at length. Much of what he said was unintelligible, but we understood that there was a considerable population on the windward side of the island, and that little was to be had in the way of refreshment on this side.

Presently they rose, giving us to understand that they would fetch others of their countrymen. We were in no position to be lavish with gifts, but Captain Bligh presented them with some buttons from his coat, which they accepted stolidly and then departed.

As soon as they had gone, Mr. Bligh made a collection of whatever small articles we could spare from our personal belongings, to be used in trade with the Indians. We gave buttons, handkerchiefs, clasp knives, buckles, and the like. Mr. Bligh also prepared us for defense. Fryer and five others were to remain in the launch in readiness for any emergency. The master had one of our cutlasses, and the others were to be carried by Bligh, Purcell, and Cole, the strongest men of the shore party; the rest of us cut clubs for ourselves, but these were to be kept hidden in the cavern, and, if possible, our trading was to be done directly in front of the cavern, so that we should always have the Indians before us.

There were, then, thirteen of us on shore, with six men in the launch at a distance of one hundred and fifty yards. We should have been glad to keep the parties closer together, but Mr. Bligh thought best to have the shore party where it could not be surrounded, and we had the launch in view so we could watch over the situation there. Thus prepared, we waited with anxiety for the arrival of visitors.

They were not long in coming. I had often remarked, at Otaheite, with what mysterious rapidity news spreads among the Indians. So it was here;

scarcely an hour had passed before twenty or thirty men had come down the cliffs; others came by canoes which they carried up the beach, and by the middle of the afternoon there were forty or fifty people in the cove. They were like the natives we had seen at Annamooka, well-set-up, hardy-looking men, with a somewhat insolent bearing; but we were relieved to see that they were unarmed, and their intent appeared peaceable enough. They were going back and forth continually, now squatting on the beach looking at the launch, now returning to the cavern to look at us. Of food and water they had little, but before evening we had bought a dozen of breadfruit, and several gallons of water. By means of Captain Bligh's magnifying glass we made a fire near the mouth of the cavern, where we cooked some of the breadfruit for our immediate needs, the natives looking on and commenting, in what appeared to be a derisive manner, on our method of doing so. No women were amongst them, nor any of their chief men, but they gave us to understand that one of these latter would visit us the next day.

Shortly after sunset they began to leave the cove, and the last of them had gone before darkness came on. This was an encouraging circumstance; for had they intended mischief, we thought, they would certainly have remained to attack us in the night. We supped upon a quarter of a breadfruit per man, and a glass of water, in better spirits than we had been at any time since the mutiny. A guard was set at the entrance of the cavern, and the rest retired to sleep, comforted by Captain Bligh's assurance that the morrow would be our last day in this dismal spot.

CHAPTER III

CAPTAIN BLIGH had the enviable faculty of being able
to compose his mind for sleep under almost any conditions. I have known him to go without rest for
seventy-two hours together; but when a suitable occasion offered, he could close his eyes and fall at once
into a refreshing slumber, though he knew that he
must be awakened a quarter of an hour later. On
this night he could hope for an undisturbed rest, and
scarcely had he lain down when his quiet breathing
assured me that he was asleep. As for myself, I was
never more wakeful, and presently left the cavern
to join the sentinels outside. They were stationed
twenty or thirty yards apart, so that they might command a view in whatever direction. It was a beautiful night, and the cove, flooded with moonlight,
seemed an enchanted spot. To the north lay the
open sea, at peace now, for the wind had died away
toward sunset. The long swells swept majestically in,
breaking first along the sides of the cove, the two
waves advancing swiftly toward each other and meeting near the centre of the beach, where the silvery
foam was thrown high in air.

As I looked about me I was reminded of certain lonely coves I had seen along the Cornish coast, on just such nights, and I found it hard to realize how vast an ocean separated us from home.

Mr. Cole was in charge of the guard; he stood in the deep shadow of a tree not far from the cavern. I had a great liking for the boatswain; we had been friends almost from the day the *Bounty* left Spithead, and there was no more competent and reliable seaman in the ship's company. He was a devout man, with a childlike trust in God which only exceeded his trust in Captain Bligh. He never for a moment doubted the captain's ability to carry us safely through whatever perils might await us. It comforted me to talk with him, and when I returned to the cave it was in a more hopeful frame of mind.

I had a fixed belief in the treacherous nature of the misnamed Friendly Islanders, and fully expected we should be attacked during the night. I, of course, kept my misgivings to myself, and the following morning they seemed a little absurd. We were astir at dawn, and there was a feeling of hopefulness and good cheer throughout the company. We even looked forward with pleasure to the return of the Indians; knowing now our needs, we felt that they would supply them, and that we should be able to leave the cove by early afternoon.

The sun was two hours high before the first of the natives came down the cliffs at the back of the cove;

and shortly afterwards two canoes arrived, with a
dozen or fifteen men in each. We were greatly disappointed to find that they had brought only a
meagre supply of provisions; we were, however, able
to purchase a little water and half a dozen breadfruit.
One of the canoe parties treated us with great insolence. They had with them half a dozen calabashes
filled with water, — much more than enough for their
own needs during the day, — but they refused to trade
for any part of it. They well knew that we were on
short rations of water, and taunted us by drinking
deeply of their own supply while we stood looking
on. Fortunately it was Nelson and not Bligh who
was attempting to trade with this party. Bligh had
little of the diplomat in his character, and had he
been present his temper might have gotten the better
of him; but Nelson remained cool and affable, and,
seeing that nothing was to be gotten from these
men, soon left them to themselves.

Upon returning to the cavern, we found Bligh trying to converse with a party, headed by an elderly
chief, which had just arrived from inland. The chief
was a stern-looking old man, well over six feet, whose
robe of tapa cloth, draped in graceful folds about his
person, proclaimed his rank; but had he been naked
he could have been recognized at once as a man of
superior station. In one hand he carried a spear of
ironwood, barbed with bones of the stingray's tail,
and tucked into a fold of his robe at the waist was

what appeared to be a comb with long wooden teeth. Bligh looked around with relief at our approach.

"You have come in good time, Nelson; I was about to send for you. See what you can make of this man's speech."

Nelson then addressed him in the Otaheitian language, while most of our company and between thirty and forty of the natives stood looking on. The chief replied with a natural grace and eloquence common to the Indians of the South Sea, but there was a look of cruelty and cunning in his eye that belied his manner. I gave him close attention, but although I somewhat prided myself upon my knowledge of the Otaheitian tongue, I found it of little use to me in listening to the Friendly Island speech. Nelson, however, had a quick ear to detect affinities and an agile mind to grasp at meanings, and it was plain that he and the chief could make themselves fairly well understood. Presently he turned to Bligh.

"He has either seen us at Annamooka or had heard of our being there," he said. "I can understand only about half of what he says, but he wishes to know how we lost the ship, and where."

We were prepared for that question. Mr. Bligh had at first been undecided how to account for our presence here, in case Indians should be met with. We could not hope to be believed if we should say that the ship was at hand, for they could see for themselves that she was not; therefore, he instructed us to say that the vessel had been lost, and that we alone had been saved from the wreck. This, we knew, was a dangerous confession to make, but circumstances forced it upon us.

I watched the man's face while Nelson was relating the story, but he remained impassive, showing neither interest in nor concern for our plight. Nelson was puzzled for a time by the man's next inquiry, but at length grasped the meaning of it.

"He wishes to see the thing with which you bring fire from the sun," he said. Bligh was reluctant to bring forth his magnifying glass again, well knowing how the Indians would covet such a precious instrument; nevertheless, he thought it best to humour the chief. Some dry leaves were gathered and crumbled into a powder. Our visitors gathered round, looking on with intense interest whilst Bligh focused the rays of the sun upon the tinder; and when they saw smoke emerge, and the small flame appear, a murmur of astonishment ran through the crowd. The chief was determined to possess this wonder worker, and when Bligh refused him, his vexation and disappointment were only too apparent. He then asked for nails, the most acceptable article of barter with the natives of the South Sea, but the few parcels we possessed could not be parted with, and Nelson was instructed to tell him that we had none.

Whilst this conversation was taking place, other Indians were arriving, amongst them a chief whose rank appeared to be equal to, if not higher than, that of the first; he showed no deference to the older man, and we observed that the crowd of natives around us, immediately they saw him, opened a lane through their ranks so that he and his followers might approach. He was a man of about forty, of commanding presence. As he entered the open space where we stood, he glanced keenly from one to another of us. Then he walked up to Captain Bligh, but I noticed that he omitted, as the older chief had done, the ceremony of rubbing noses — a formal courtesy which had never been omitted heretofore, when we had the *Bounty* at our backs.

None of us could recollect having seen either of these chiefs at Annamooka. We learned that the name of the elder man was Macca-ackavow, — at least, that is as near as I can come to the sound of the name, — and the other was called Eefow. We gathered that both came from the island of Tongataboo. When Bligh informed them that we proposed to go to either that island or to Annamooka, Eefow offered to accompany us as soon as the wind and sea should moderate. Bligh invited them into the cavern, where he presented each with a knife and a shirt.

It was at this time that I took up one of the skulls we had found there, and, bringing it to the chief Eefow, asked, in the Otaheitian dialect, whence it came. His face lit up at the question, and he replied: "Feejee, Feejee." He then went on, with great animation, to explain about them; and we understood that he himself had been the slayer of two of these victims. Captain Bligh was greatly interested in this narration, for when he had visited the Friendly Islands with Captain Cook he had gathered much information about a great archipelago, unknown to Europeans, called "Feejee" by the Indians, and which was not far distant from the Friendly Islands. He had Nelson question Eefow at length about Feejee, and was told the group comprised a vast number of islands, the nearest of which lay about a two days' sail from Tofoa. When we came out of the cavern, Bligh had Eefow point out their direction, and the chief showed him what bearings should be taken to sail toward them from Tofoa. The direction was to the west-northwest, which confirmed what Bligh had already been told.

This conference in the cavern had gone most prosperously, and we were encouraged to hope that our fears were groundless with respect to the Indians' intentions toward us. Another favourable incident occurred at this time: A man named Nageete, whom Mr. Bligh remembered having seen at Annamooka, came forward and greeted him in the most friendly manner. Although not a chief, he appeared to be a personage of some importance, and Bligh made much of him, taking care, however, to distinguish between his attitude toward Nageete and that toward the chiefs. With this man's help we were able to add considerably to our stock of water, enough for our immediate needs, so that we could keep the launch's stock intact; and we also purchased a few more bread-fruit and a half-dozen large yams; but our scant sup-ply of articles for trade was soon exhausted. There-after they would give us nothing; not so much as half a breadfruit would they part with unless payment were made for it.

Under these circumstances, we were at a loss what to do; we had parted with everything we could spare and were still in great need of food and water. Bligh appealed to the chiefs, again explaining our predica-ment. Nelson was as eloquent as possible, but the effect was negligible.

When he had finished, Macca-ackavow replied: "You say you have nothing left, but you have the instrument for making fire. Let me have that and my people here shall give you all they have."

But this request Bligh could not, of course, comply with; we had no flint and steel amongst us, and none of us was able to kindle fire by friction, in the Indian fashion. Macca-ackavow became sullen at our re-fusal to part with the magnifying glass.

Eefow then said: "Let us see what you have in your boat." But again Bligh refused, for the few tools and parcels of nails we had there were only less nec-essary than food itself.

So matters went until toward midday.

For our dinner we had each a small piece of cooked

breadfruit, and a sliver of pork. Bligh invited the
chiefs to join our meal, which they did. It was a
most uncomfortable repast. We were all sensible of
a change in the attitude of the Indians: small groups
conferred among themselves, and the two chiefs,
whilst eating with us, conversed in what appeared to
be some special and figurative speech, so that not even
Nelson could understand a word that was said.

Fifteen of our company were on shore at this
time; Fryer, with three men, remained with the
launch, which still lay at a grapnel just beyond the
break of the surf. We estimated that there were
well over two hundred Indians around us, and not a
woman amongst them. Fortunately, only the chiefs
and two or three of their immediate retainers were
armed.

The chiefs now left us and went amongst their
people. Bligh took the occasion to inform us of his
plans and to instruct us as to what our behaviour
toward the natives should be throughout the afternoon.

"It is not yet clear," he said, "that they have formed
a design against us, and we must act as though we
had no suspicion of any such intent; but be on your
guard, every man of you. . . . Mr. Peckover, you
shall select three men and carry what supplies we have
to the launch; but perform this business in a casual
manner. Let there be no haste in your actions. We
shall leave the cove at sunset, whether or no Eefow

accompanies us, and make our way to Tongataboo, but I wish the Indians to be deceived on this point until we are ready to embark."

We had a fire going near the cavern, and the bread-fruit had been cooked as we bought it. Peckover chose Peter Lenkletter, Lebogue, and young Tinkler to assist him, and they now began carrying down the supplies, a little at a time. This was dangerous work, for they had to run the gantlet of many groups of savages collected between us and the launch, and it was performed with a coolness deserving of high praise. Tinkler, who was no more than a lad, behaved admirably, and he was immensely proud that he had been chosen for the task over the other midshipmen. Meanwhile, Bligh sat at the mouth of the cavern, keeping a watchful eye upon all that went on and, at the same time, writing in his journal as quietly as though he were in his cabin on the *Bounty*. The rest of us busied ourselves with small matters, to make it appear that we expected to spend the night ashore. Nageete, who had strolled away after our midday meal, returned after a little time, apparently as well disposed as ever. He asked what our intentions were, and was told that we should wait until Eefow was ready to accompany us to Tongataboo, but that we hoped, in case the weather favoured, he would consent to go on the following day.

Nageete then said: "Eefow will go if you will give him the fire maker; and you should let him have it, rather than Macca-ackavow, for he is the greater chief."

Bligh might have resorted to guile, making a promise of the coveted glass, but this he refused to do, telling Nageete that under no circumstances could he part with it.

Presently the two chiefs rejoined us, and Bligh, with Nelson to interpret, questioned them further about the Feejee Islands, doing everything possible to keep our relations with them on a friendly and casual footing.

Whilst this conversation was taking place, an incident occurred that might easily have proved disastrous. There was a great crowd of Indians along the beach. Of a sudden, a dozen or more of them rushed to the line which held the launch to the shore and began to haul it in. We heard a warning shout from Peckover, who was just then returning with his party. Bligh, cutlass in hand, rushed for the beach, the rest of us, including the chiefs, following. His courage and force of character never showed to better advantage than on this occasion. We were vastly outnumbered, and might easily have been attacked and slain; but Bligh so overawed them by his manner that they immediately let go the rope, and Fryer and those with him hauled the launch back to its former position. This move of the Indians was made, I think, without the knowledge of the chiefs. However that may be, they at least ordered the men away from that vicinity, — Bligh having insisted upon this, — and all became quiet again.

It would have been well could we have embarked then and there; and Bligh would have had us make a rush for it, I think, had it not been that Cole and three others had been sent inland in the hope of finding a few more quarts of water. They had not yet returned, so we made our way back to the cavern to wait for them.

Then followed an anxious time. It became more and more apparent that we were to be attacked, and that the savages were merely biding a favourable opportunity. We were equally sure that the chiefs were of one mind about this and that they had informed their followers that we were to be destroyed.

"Keep well together, lads," said Bligh quietly. "See that none of them comes behind us. Damn their eyes! What are they waiting for?"

"I believe they're afraid of us, sir," said Fryer. "Either that, or they hope to take us by surprise."

We had not long to wait for evidence of their intentions. Savages, although they invariably recognize and respect the authority of their chiefs, lack discipline, and when a course of action is decided upon, are impatient to put it into effect. So it was here. Shortly after this, we heard, from a distance, an ominous sound: the knocking of stones together, which we rightly supposed was a signal amongst them previous to an attack. At first only a few of them did this, but gradually the sound spread, increasing in volume, to all parts of the cove; at moments it became all but deafening, and then would die away only to be resumed with even greater insistence, as though the commoners were growing increasingly impatient with their chiefs for withholding the signal for slaughter. The effect upon our little band may be imagined. We believed that our last hour had come; we stood together, a well-knit band, every man resolved to sell his life as dearly as possible.

It was late afternoon when Cole and his party returned with about two quarts of water which they had collected amongst the rocks. Mr. Bligh had kept a record of everything we had been able to secure in the way of provision, and the water we had either bought or found for ourselves had been just sufficient for our needs. We had added nothing to our twenty-eight gallons in the launch, but neither had we taken anything from that supply. Now that the shore party was again united, we waited only for a suitable opportunity before making an attempt to embark. Meanwhile, the clapping of stones went on, now here, now there, and yet it was necessary for us to keep up the pretense that we suspected nothing.

Nageete, who had been with us during this time, was becoming increasingly restless and was only seeking some pretext for getting away, but Bligh kept him engaged in conversation. We were all gathered before the entrance of the cavern in such a way that the Indians could not pass behind us. For the most part, they were gathered in groups of twenty or thirty, at some distance, and we saw the two chiefs passing from group to group. Presently they returned to where we stood, and I must do them the credit to say that they were masters at the art of dissembling. We asked them the meaning of the stone clapping, and they gave us to understand that it was merely a game in which their followers indulged to while away the time. They then attempted to persuade Captain Bligh and Nelson to accompany them away from the rest of us, as though they wished to confer with him in private, but Bligh pretended not to understand. We were all on our feet, in instant readiness to defend ourselves; nevertheless, I believe that we did succeed by our actions — for a time at least — in convincing the chiefs that we were ignorant of their intentions. Immediately they returned to us the clapping of stones had ceased, and the ensuing silence seemed the more profound.

Eefow then asked: "You will sleep on shore tonight?"

Captain Bligh replied: "No, I never sleep away from my boat, but it may be that I shall leave a part of my men in the cavern."

Our hope was, of course, that we could persuade the Indians of an intention to remain in the cove until the following day. I think there must have been a difference of opinion between the two chiefs as to when the attack upon us should be made, and that the elder one was for immediate action and Eefow for a night attack. They again conversed together in their figurative speech, of which we understood nothing.

Bligh said to us, very quietly: "Be ready, lads. If they make a hostile move, we will kill them both and fight our way to the launch."

We were, of course, in the unfortunate position of not being able to begin the attack, and yet we were almost at the point where action, however desperate, would have seemed preferable to further delay.

Eefow now turned again to Nelson. "Tell your captain," he said, "that we shall spend the night here. To-morrow I will go with you in your boat to Tonga-taboo."

Nelson interpreted this message, and Bligh replied: "That is good."

The chiefs then left us; but when they had gone a distance of fifteen or twenty paces, Macca-ackavow turned with an expression on his face that I shall not soon forget.

"You will not spend the night ashore?" he again asked.

"What does he say, Nelson?" asked Bligh.

Nelson interpreted.

"God damn him, tell him no!" said Bligh.

Nelson conveyed this message at some length, and in a more diplomatic manner than Bligh had used. The chief stood facing us, glancing swiftly from side to side amongst his followers. Then he again spoke, very briefly; and having done so, strode swiftly away.

"What is it, Nelson?" asked Bligh.

Nelson smiled grimly. "*'Te mo maté gimotoloo,'*" he replied. "Their intentions are clear enough now. It means: 'Then you shall die.'"

Bligh's actions at this time were beyond praise. To see him rise to a desperate occasion was an experience to be treasured in the memory. He was cool and clear-headed, and he talked quietly, even cheerfully, to us.

"It is now or never, lads," he said. "Hall, serve out quickly the water Mr. Cole has brought in."

The calabash was passed rapidly from hand to hand, for we knew it would be impossible to get the water to the launch; each man had a generous sup, and it was needed, for we had been on short rations for three days. All this while Bligh had kept a firm grip with his left hand on Nageete's arm, holding his cutlass in his right. He was determined that, if we were to die, Nageete should die with us. The man's face was a study. I have not been able to determine in my own mind, to this day, whether he was playing a part or was genuinely friendly towards us. I imagine, however, that he had a heart as treacherous as those of his countrymen.

Bligh had already instructed us in what order we should proceed to the beach. Cole, also armed with a cutlass, took his station with the captain on the other side of Nageete; and the rest of us fell in behind, with Purcell and Norton bringing up the rear.

"Forward, lads!" said Bligh. "Let these bastards see how Englishmen behave in a tight place!"

We then proceeded toward the beach, everyone in a kind of silent horror.

I believe it was the promptness, the unexpectedness of our action alone that saved us. Had we shown the least hesitation, we must have all been slain; but Bligh led us straight on, directly toward one large group of Indians who were between us and the launch. They parted to let us through, and I well remember my feeling of incredulous wonder at finding myself still alive when we had passed beyond them. Not a word was spoken, nor was a hand lifted against us until we reached the beach.

Fryer had, of course, seen us coming, and had slacked away until the launch was within half a dozen paces of the beach, in about four feet of water.

"In with you, lads! Look alive!" Bligh shouted. "Purcell, stand by with me — you and Norton!"

Within half a minute we were all in the boat, save Bligh and the two men with him. Nageete now wrenched himself free from Bligh's grasp and ran up the beach. The captain and Purcell made for the boat, wisely not attempting to bring in the grapnel on shore; but Norton, who Bligh thought was immediately behind him, ran back to fetch it. We shouted to him to let it go; but either he did not or would not hear.

The Indians by this time had been roused to action, and they were upon Norton in an instant, beating out his brains with stones. Meanwhile we had hauled Bligh and Purcell into the boat and got out the oars. The natives seized the line which held us to the shore; but Bligh severed it with a stroke of his cutlass, and the men forward quickly hauled us out to the other grapnel and attempted to pull it up. To our dismay, one of the flukes had caught and two or three precious minutes were lost before it was gotten clear. It was fortunate for us that the savages were unarmed; had they been possessed of spears, or bows and arrows, the chance of any man's escaping would have been small indeed. The only spears amongst them were those carried by the two chiefs. Macca-ackavow hurled his, which passed within a few inches of Peckover's head and fell into the water a dozen yards beyond us.

But whilst they had no man-made weapons, the beach offered them an inexhaustible supply of stones, and we received such a shower of these that, had we not been a good thirty yards distant, a number of us might have met Norton's fate. As it was, Purcell was knocked senseless by a blow on the head, and various others were badly hurt. The speed and accuracy with which they cast the stones were amazing. We protected ourselves as well as we could with bundles of cloathing which we held before us.

Meanwhile the men forward were hauling desperately on the grapnel, which at last gave way and came up with one fluke broken. Bligh, at the tiller, was in the most exposed position of any; that he escaped serious injury was due to the efforts of Elphinstone and Cole, who shielded him with floor boards from the stern sheets.

We now began to pull away from them, but the treacherous villains were not done with us yet. They got one of their canoes into the water, which they loaded with stones, whereupon a dozen of them leaped into her to pursue us. Our six men at the oars pulled with all their strength, but we were so heavily laden that the savages gained swiftly upon us. Nevertheless, we had got out of the cove and beyond view of the throng on the beach before we were overtaken. They now had us at their mercy, and began throwing stones with such deadly accuracy that it seemed a miracle some of us were not killed. A few of the stones fell into the boat and were hurled back at them; we had the satisfaction of seeing one of their paddlers struck squarely in the face by a stone cast by the boatswain. However, that was a chance shot; we should have been no match for them at this kind of warfare even had we possessed a supply of ammunition.

In the hope of distracting their attention from us, Mr. Bligh threw some articles of cloathing into the water; and to our joy they stopped to take them in.

It was now getting dark, and, as they could have had but a few stones left in the canoe, they gave over the attack, and a moment later disappeared past the headland at the entrance to the cove. We were by no means sure that others would not attempt to come after us, so we pulled straight out to sea until we caught the breeze. With our sails set, we were soon past all danger of pursuit.

I was busy during the next hour caring for our wounded, of whom there were nine in all. Purcell was badly hurt. He had been struck a glancing blow on the head, which laid open his scalp and knocked him unconscious, but, by the time I was able to attend to him, he was again sitting up, apparently but little the worse for a blow that would have killed most men. An examination of the wound assured me pretty well that the skull had not been fractured. It was necessary to take half a dozen stitches in the scalp. Elphinstone had had two fingers of his right hand broken while protecting Captain Bligh, and Lenkletter had been deeply gashed across the cheek bone. The other wounds were bruises, the worst being that of Hall, who had been struck full on the right breast and nearly knocked out of the launch.

It can be imagined with what feelings of gratitude to God we watched the island of Tofoa dropping away astern. Now that we had time to reflect, a truer sense of the horror of the situation from which we had so narrowly escaped came home to us. The death of Norton cast a gloom upon all our spirits, but we avoided speaking of him then; the manner of his death was too clearly in mind, and it seemed that we could still hear the yells of the savages who had murdered him. Captain Bligh took his loss very much to heart and blamed himself that he had not thought to inform us, beforehand, to give no heed to the grapnel on shore. But he was by no means at fault. What the situation would be on the beach could not have been foretold, and poor Norton himself should have seen the folly of trying to save the grapnel. Nevertheless, his was an act of heroism such as few men would have been capable of attempting.

The wind, from the east-southeast, freshened as we drew away from the land; the darkness deepened, and soon Tofoa was lost to view save for the baleful glare from its volcano, reflected on the clouds above. Meanwhile we had gotten the boat in order and had taken the places Captain Bligh had assigned to us for the night. With respect to food, we still had our one hundred and fifty pounds of bread, short of a few ounces eaten at Tofoa, twenty pounds of pork, thirty-one coconuts, sixteen breadfruit, and seven yams; but both the breadfruit and the yams, which had been cooked on shore, had been trampled under our feet during the attack. Nevertheless, we salvaged the filthy mess and ate it during subsequent days. As already related, we still had twenty-eight gallons of water — the same amount we had carried away from the *Bounty* — but we had left only three bottles of wine, and five quarts of rum.

I am not likely to forget the conference we then held to determine our future course of action. We were running, of necessity, before the wind, in a direction almost the opposite to that of Annamooka or Tongataboo, and Fryer, who was the first to speak, earnestly begged Captain Bligh to continue this course — to proceed with us in the direction of home.

"We know what we have to expect of the savages, sir," he said. "Without arms, our experience at Tofoa will only be repeated on other islands, and we could not hope to come off so fortunate again."

Other voices were joined to the master's; there was no doubt as to the general desire of our company to brave the perils of the sea rather than those certain to be met with on land. Bligh was willing to be persuaded; in fact, I am sure that he himself would have proposed this change of plan had no one else spoken of it. Nevertheless, he wished us to be fully aware of the dangers ahead of us.

"Do you know, Mr. Fryer," he asked, "how far we must sail before we shall have any expectation of help?"

"Not exactly, sir."

"To the Dutch East Indies," Bligh went on; "and the first of their settlements is on the island of Timor, a full twelve hundred leagues from here."

A moment of silence followed. Not one of us, I believe, but was thinking: "Twelve hundred leagues! What hope, then, have we?"

"Even so," said Bligh, "our situation is by no means hopeless. Granted that every man of you gives me his full support, I believe we shall reach Timor."

"That you shall have, sir!" said Peckover. "What do you say, lads?"

There was a hearty agreement to this.

"Very well," said Bligh. "Now let me tell you, briefly, what we are likely to have in store. First, as to favouring elements: we are at a most fortunate time of year; we can count upon easterly winds for as long as we shall be at sea. The northwest monsoon should not commence before November, and long before that time we shall have reached Timor, or be forever past the need of reaching it. The launch is stoutly built; deeply laden as we are, we need not fear her ability to run before the wind. Her performance at this moment is a promise of what she can do. As to the perils we must meet —"

He paused while reflecting upon them. "Of those I need not speak," he went on. "They are known to all of you. But this I will say: If we are to reach Timor, we must live upon a daily allowance of food and water no more than sufficient to preserve our lives. I desire every man's assurance that he will cheerfully agree to the amount I shall decide upon. It will be small indeed, but we can be almost certain of replenishing our water many times before the end of the voyage. However, that remains to be seen, and I shall not anticipate doing so in deciding what each man's portion shall be. Mr. Fryer, have I your solemn promise to abide by my judgment in this matter?"

"Yes, sir," Fryer replied promptly.

Mr. Bligh then called each man by name, and all agreed as Fryer had done.

These matters having been decided, we fell silent, and so remained for some time; then Cole, who was seated amidships, said: "Mr. Bligh, we should be pleased if you would ask God's blessing upon our voyage."

"That I shall do, Mr. Cole," Bligh replied.

Never, I imagine, have English seamen been more sensible of the need for Divine guidance than the eighteen men in the *Bounty's* launch. We waited, our heads bowed in the darkness, for our leader to speak.

"Almighty God. Thou seest our afflictions. Thou knowest our need. Grant that we may quit ourselves like men in the trials and dangers that lie before us. Watch over us. Strengthen our hearts; and in Thy divine mercy and compassion, bring us all in safety to the haven toward which we now direct our course. Amen."

The watch for the early part of the night was now set, and the rest of us arranged ourselves for sleep as well as we could. The wind blew with increasing freshness, but the launch behaved well. The moonlit sea before us seemed to stretch away to infinity.

"Slack away a little, Mr. Cole," Bligh called.

CHAPTER IV

THE sea was calm, though there was a fresh breeze at east. Now that Tofoa had been lost to view, every man in the boat, I believe, felt, for the first time since casting off from the *Bounty*, a faint thrill of hope. I was fully aware of the immense remoteness of the Dutch East Indies, and of the difficulties and dangers through which we should be obliged to pass were we to reach those distant islands; but Mr. Bligh's confident manner, and his calmness during our perilous escape from the savages, convinced me of our good fortune in being under his command.

Heavily laden as she was, and with only the reefed lug foresail set, the boat sailed fast to the westward. Mr. Bligh was at the tiller, with Peckover beside him; Fryer, Elphinstone, Nelson, and I sat in the stern sheets. The two midshipmen on the thwart were already asleep; but Tinkler, who had been chosen for Peckover's watch, was making prodigious efforts to keep awake. The gunner noticed the lad's yawns.

"Get you to sleep, Mr. Tinkler," he said gruffly; "I shan't need you to-night."

There was little talk among the men forward,

though nearly all were awake. The slower-witted, I suppose, were only now arriving at a full realization of what lay before us. I heard frequent groans from those who were nursing bruises, and indeed my own injured shoulder was so painful as to preclude the possibility of sleep. It may be worthy of remark that the tincture of *Arnica montana,* of which I had a small supply, proved of great value to those of us who had been hurt.

Calm as the sea was, the launch was so deep that we shipped quantities of water as we ran clear of the land and began to feel the long roll of the Southern Ocean from east to west. Peckover set two men — Lebogue and Simpson — to bailing. Toward midnight, as the sea grew higher, they had all they could do to keep her clear of water, and became so fatigued that Peckover ordered others to relieve them. He pulled out his large silver watch, scrutinized it intently, and returned it to his pocket.

"What hour have you, Mr. Peckover?" asked the captain.

"I can't make out, sir."

Bligh glanced up at the stars. "Mr. Fryer, you have had no sleep?" he asked.

"Not yet, sir."

"Take the tiller, if you please; I shall try to rest, and I recommend you to do the same at four o'clock."

They changed places, moving gingerly in the pitching boat, and Bligh made himself as comfortable as possible. Hayward and Hallet rubbed their eyes as they were wakened to their turns at the bailing; they drew their jackets around them, shivering at the spray which flew constantly over the quarters.

Toward morning the wind chopped round from N.E. to E.S.E., and blew very cold, while the sea grew high and confused, breaking frequently over the stern of the launch. Mr. Bligh was aware of the change instantly, and took the tiller from the master's hands. Four men were now required to throw out the water, which came in sheets over the transom and quarters of the boat. At dawn the sky was overcast with low, dirty clouds, scudding fast to the westward, and the sun rose red and ominous. We were a sorry crew in the light of this Sunday morning; haggard-eyed, wet to the skin with salt spray, and so stiff that some could scarcely straighten their legs. Nelson tried to smile; his teeth chattered so violently that he stammered when he spoke.

Mr. Bligh's face looked drawn in the gray light, but his eyes were cool and alert. Each wave sent sheets of wind-driven spray into the boat; presently a sea greater than the others swung us high and curled over the transom. Above the roaring of the waves I heard faint cries and curses from the men as a rush of water swept forward in the bilges. Then, while I plied a coconut shell, snatched up in an instant, I heard Bligh's voice, audible in the calm of the trough.

He was shouting to Hall, who sat with Lamb in the bows:—

"The bread! The bread!"

The man had been crouching with his head in his arms, shivering with the cold. He stared aft dazedly. Our bread had been stowed in the bow of the launch, the place least exposed to the driving spray. It was in three bags, and had been covered with the spare mainsail.

"Aye, aye, sir!" Hall shouted back, bending down to raise the canvas and examine what was beneath. A moment later he straightened his back. "One sack is wet, sir!" he shouted. "The lot will be spoiled if it's left here!"

Bligh glanced fore and aft. "Mr. Purcell!" he called.

The carpenter was plying a scoop close beside his chest. Another wave was passing beneath us, bringing fresh sheets of spray, but no solid water this time. He passed the scoop to the man behind him, who began to bail at once.

"Aye, sir," he said.

"Clear your chest of tools; place them in the bilges."

The carpenter removed the tray of small tools, and the heavier ones beneath.

"Now, lads, look alive!" Bligh shouted when all was ready. "Wait till I give the word. One sack at a time! Hall, you and Smith pull out the first and pass it to Lebogue! Then aft to the chest, hand to hand. Mr. Hayward, open the chest when the time comes. Mr. Purcell will cut the seizing and dump the bread in loose. Work fast! It 'll be empty bellies otherwise!"

All but those bailing waited in suspense until the launch's bow shot up and she jogged back into the next trough.

"Now!" shouted Bligh.

Off came the sail; the sack was passed swiftly aft from hand to hand, cut open with a touch of the carpenter's clasp knife, and dumped into the open chest. Hayward closed the lid with a snap. The sail was safely tucked about the two remaining sacks before we felt the lift of the following wave. In the momentary lulls between succeeding waves, the other sacks came aft and their contents were safely stowed.

Every man in the boat, I believe, must have drawn a sigh of heartfelt relief. Small as our supply of bread was for such a voyage as lay before us, it was all that stood between us and certain death by starvation. It had been stowed in the chest not a moment too soon.

The seas grew so high that our scrap of sail hung slack from the yard when in the trough, filling with a report like a musket shot as the following sea raised us high aloft. Then the launch would rush forward dizzily, while water poured in over the quarters, and the straining sail, small as it was, threatened to snap

the unstayed mast. Mr. Bligh crouched at the helm
with an impassive face, turning his head mechanically
to glance back as each rearing sea overtook us. Had
he relaxed his vigilance for a moment, or made a false
motion of the tiller, the boat would have broached
to and filled instantly. All hands were now obliged
to bail, those who had nothing better throwing out
the water with coconut shells. We were greatly
hampered by the coils of rope, spare sails, and bundles
of cloathing in the bilges.

The force of the gale increased as it veered back
to east and to northeast; it was soon apparent to all
hands that our sail was too much to have set.

"We must lighten her, Mr. Fryer!" Bligh shouted
above the roar of wind and sea. "Each man may keep
two suits of cloathing — jettison the rest! And
heave overboard the spare foresail and all but one
coil of rope!"

"Aye, sir!" replied the master. "Can we not
shorten sail? I fear we'll drive her under with but
a single reef!"

Bligh shook his head. "No, she'll do. Over with
the spare gear!"

His orders were carried out with an alacrity which
showed that those under him realized the imminence
of our danger. Though the weight of what we cast
away would scarcely have exceeded that of a heavy
man, the boat rode better for it, and the clearing
of the bilges enabled six of us, bailing constantly, to

keep her dry. A quarter of a cooked breadfruit, much dirtied and trampled during our naval engagement with the Friendly Islanders, was served out to each man with half a pint of water.

It was close on noon when the wind veered once more to E.S.E.; and as we could do nothing but run straight before it, the boat was now steered W.N.W. —in which direction, the Indians had informed us, lay the group of large islands they called Feejee. The sea was now higher than ever, and the labour of bailing very wearisome, but I was losing my dread of the boat foundering, for I perceived that since we had lightened her she rode wonderfully well, and was in little danger with a skillful hand at the helm. At twelve o'clock by the gunner's watch, Mr. Bligh had his sextant fetched out, and with two of us holding him propped up in the stern sheets, he managed to observe the altitude of the sun. Elphinstone was at the tiller, and I noticed with relief that he steered with confidence and skill. Our lives, from moment to moment, depended upon our helmsman. Had there been an awkward or timid man in his place, our chances would have been small indeed.

"We have done well," said the captain, when he had returned to the stern sheet. . . . "Ah, well steered, Mr. Elphinstone! Damme! Well steered!"

A great sea lifted us high and passed under the launch, roaring and foaming on both sides. As we dropped into the calm of the trough, Mr. Bligh went on: "You see how she behaves, lads? She'll see us through if we do our part! By God, she will! Mr. Fryer, by my reckoning, we have run eighty-six miles since leaving Tofoa."

The wind was our friend as well as our enemy. Captain Bligh's feeling for the launch was shared by every man of us; we were beginning to love her, now that we knew something of her qualities.

"We must have a log," Bligh added. "Mr. Fryer, I count on you and the boatswain to provide us with a line, properly marked. Mr. Purcell, see what you can do to make us a log chip."

When we had eaten our dinner of five small coconuts, the carpenter took apart the tray from his chest; and from its bottom—a piece of thin oaken plank—he sawed out a small triangle, about six inches on a side. One side was weighted with a bit of sheet lead, and a hole was bored at each corner. The whole made what seamen call a "chip."

We had on board two stout fishing lines, each of about fifty fathoms length. One was kept towing behind the boat with a hook to which a bit of rag had been made fast. From the other, Fryer made a bridle for the log chip, measured off twelve fathoms, and marked the place with his thumb. The boatswain had been twisting some bits of a handkerchief; as the master held out the line, he roved a bit of the rag through the strands and knotted it fast. Then, with the carpenter's rule, Fryer measured off very carefully twenty-five feet. At this point the boat-swain made fast another bit of rag, with a trailing end, in which he tied one knot. This was repeated, tying two knots, three knots, and so on until there were eight knots in the last rag.

"Will eight be enough, sir?" Fryer asked.

The captain was at the tiller, glancing back over his shoulder at the wave behind us. When it had passed under us, he replied in the sudden calm: "Aye, eight will do. Mr. Peckover, take your watch in the lee of the chest there, and practise counting seconds with Mr. Cole. You'll soon have the hang of it, I'll be bound!"

I heard them for a long time, as we sank into the troughs between the seas, counting monotonously: "One-an', two-an', three-an', four-an' . . ." At last the gunner called back: "Mr. Bligh!"

"Aye; are you ready?"

"We'll not be a second off, sir!"

"Then heave the log!"

Peckover coiled the line in his right hand to pay out freely, while the boatswain took his place at the star-board quarter. At a sign from the gunner he cast the log chip into the sea, and as the twelve-fathom mark passed through his fingers he began to count. At the fifteenth second he gripped the line and turned to Mr. Bligh.

"Four and a half, sir," he reported, beginning to pull in the line.

"Good! From now on, let the mate of the watch heave the log every hour. I shall reckon our longitude each day with the aid of Mr. Peckover's watch, and we can check the results by dead reckoning."

Crouched in the stern sheets, shivering and wet to the skin, I caught Nelson's eye as I turned my back to the spray. His thoughts, perhaps, like my own, were of the change in Bligh. He was above all a man of action, and seemed happy only in situations which demanded the exercise of his truly great qualities of skill, courage and resourcefulness. He was born to lead men in peril or in battle, and now, in the boat, with the sea for enemy and his task the preservation of his men's lives, he was at his best — cheerful, kindly, and considerate to a degree I should have believed impossible a fortnight before.

The weather continued very severe during the afternoon and throughout the night; Captain Bligh held the tiller for eighteen hours. Though we had not yet begun to suffer greatly for lack of food, the night was a miserable one. At sunset the wind veered a little to the southward and blew so chill that I found it impossible to sleep. Laborious as the task of bailing was, we seized the scoops gladly when our turns came, for the hard work warmed us.

By nine o'clock the wind had blown the sky clear; the moon, sinking toward the west, cast a cold, serene light on the roaring sea. Each time the boat was flung aloft, we gazed out over miles of angry water, tossing, breaking, and ridged with great waves running to the west. Had not every bone in my body ached with the cold, I think I might have felt a kind of exultation at the majesty of the spectacle, and in the thought that our boat, small and frail as she was, could carry us safely over such a sea. And I was aware of what might be termed a cosmic rhythm in the procession of the waves. They passed under us with great regularity, the interval being about the time it took me to count ten, very slowly; they seemed to be about two hundred yards from crest to crest, and I estimated that they passed us at not less than thirty miles an hour. Hour after hour we alternated between fierce wind and spray and the roar of breaking water on the crests, and the calm of the black troughs, where the launch all but lost steerageway.

Mr. Bligh was silent during the night; his task was too exacting to permit of speech. He must have suffered more than any of us, for the movements required to steer the boat were too slight to warm his blood. The moon, sinking ever lower ahead of us, shone full on his face; his expression was calm and alert, though he could not suppress a strong shuddering.

At last the moon went down on our larboard bow. The stars shone with the cold light of an autumn evening at home. The waves roaring about us broke in sheets of pale fire, so that at times I could distinguish the faces of my companions in the eerie light.

Nelson and I had returned to the stern sheets after a long trick with the bails. We were in the calm between two seas at the time. Glancing over the side, I saw swift shapes of fire gliding back and forth alongside the boat: a dozen, a score of them — darting ahead, veering this way and that, disappearing under the boat. One of them came to the surface within a yard of us, snorted loudly, and shot ahead.

"Porpoises!" Nelson exclaimed.

"Aye," said the captain; "my mouth waters at the thought of a porpoise steak, no matter how raw!"

Gripping the gunwales, we gazed over the side, thinking less of the beauty of the phosphorescent tracks than of the abundance of food so near at hand — food we were powerless to secure. The seas overtook us with a regularity that lightened Bligh's task at the tiller. He seemed not to feel the piercing chill of the air that penetrated our drenched cloathes. The splendid performance of the launch engaged his whole attention. Though trembling with cold, I caught something of his own exhilaration as I watched the great seas rearing their backs in the starlight and sweeping toward us.

"How well she rides!" said Nelson, between chattering teeth.

"I watched her building," Bligh replied proudly; "I inspected every strake and frame that went into her! A stancher boat was never built! Were she decked and reasonably laden, I could take her round the world."

When our turn came to bail once more, my legs were so benumbed that I had difficulty in getting forward, and Nelson had to be helped to his feet. The sky was turning gray when we were relieved once more.

The captain ordered a teaspoonful of rum to be served out. This revived us wonderfully, and we breakfasted on some bits of cooked yam found in the bottom of the boat. The weather was abating, although the sea would still have appalled a landsman, and the rising sun warmed us sufficiently to give us the use of our stiffened limbs.

By eight o'clock, when the boatswain hove the log, the wind had moderated to a fresh breeze, and so little spray was coming aboard that those forward were able to dry their cloathes. Captain Bligh glanced down at the compass and beckoned to Elphinstone.

"Take the helm," he said. "Keep her W.N.W. We should raise the land soon, unless the Indians are liars."

He flexed the muscles of his arm, stiffened by cold and his long night's work, and went on, addressing us all: "We have come through a bad night. In these latitudes, we may sail all the way to Timor without again being so sorely tried. You have borne up well, my lads, and we can depend upon the launch. My word for it! If we husband our provisions as agreed upon, we shall all reach home!"

"Never fear, sir," Cole ventured to remark. "We're with ye to a man. And thank God for Captain Bligh to lead us—eh, lads?"

There was a hearty chorus from the people: "Aye!" "Well spoken!" "Ye can lay to that!"

As the morning advanced we sighted several flocks of birds, hovering over shoals of fish—a sure indication of land. Once we passed through the midst of a school of tunnies, leaping and thrashing the sea into foam, yet none would seize our hook. We were now keeping a sharp lookout, and a little before noon land was discovered—a small flat island, bearing southwest, about four leagues distant. Other islands appeared, and by three in the afternoon we could count eight on the horizon, from south around through the west to north.

"The Feejee Islands," said Mr. Bligh, who had been awakened from a refreshing sleep by the first shout of *"Land!"* "We are the first white men to set eyes on them!"

"Can't we land here, sir?" asked the carpenter.

"Spoken like a fool, Mr. Purcell," said Bligh bluntly. "You've a short memory if you've so soon forgotten Tofoa! We could commit no greater folly than to land here. Captain Cook never saw these islands; but when I was master of the *Resolution*, in

1777, he learned much of their inhabitants from the Friendly Islanders.   They are known to be fierce and treacherous, and eaters of human flesh.   No, by God! We shall keep well clear of these fellows!"

CHAPTER V

TOWARD evening we raised three small islands to the northwest, about seven leagues distant, passing them at nightfall, when we snugged down to a reefed foresail. Had our circumstances been happier, I might have enjoyed more fully the emotion aroused by sailing an unknown sea, studded with islands on which no European had hitherto laid eyes.

Nelson was possessed of that most precious of gifts: an inquiring and philosophical turn of mind. Even in our situation, with not one chance in a thousand, as it seemed, of seeing England again, he was able to derive pleasure from the contemplation of the sea and the sky by day, and the stars by night. He regarded each island we passed, no matter how distant, with an inquiring eye, speculating as to whether it was of volcanic or of coralline formation, whether it was inhabited, and what vegetation might spring from its soil. When we passed shoals of fish, he named them, and the birds diving and hovering overhead. And what little I know of astronomy was learned from Nelson during the long nights on the *Bounty's* launch.

Though the wind freshened after dark and kept us pretty wet throughout the night, the sea was not rough and we managed to get a little sleep by putting ourselves at watch and watch, half of us sitting up, whilst the others stretched out in the boat's bottom. I found it a great luxury to be able to extend my legs, and, although shivering with cold, I slept for nearly three hours, and awoke much refreshed. At daybreak all hands seemed better than on the morning before. We breakfasted on a quarter of a pint of water each and a few bits of yam, the last of those we had found in the bottom of the boat.

During the early hours of the morning the wind moderated, and Mr. Bligh ordered the chest opened in order to examine the bread. One of the sacks was well dried, and the bread which had been wet on the first night was spread out in the sun. When it had been thoroughly dried, we carefully sorted our entire supply, placing all that was damaged or rotten in the sack, to prevent the rot from infecting what was still good. This damaged bread was to be eaten first.

After Captain Bligh had taken his observation at noon, he informed us that our latitude was eighteen degrees, ten minutes, south, and that, according to his reckoning, we had run ninety-four miles in the twenty-four hours past. It was cloudy to the westward, but Lebogue and Cole, old seamen both, believed that they could discern high land in that direction, at a place where the clouds seemed fixed.

We had been through so much since leaving the *Bounty* that I had scarcely given a thought to what I ate; now, casting up the total of what I had had in the seven days past, I perceived that the whole of it was no more than a hungry man, in the midst of plenty, would have eaten at a meal. Our scant rations had had their effect — cheeks were pinched and eyes unnaturally hollow and bright. There were no complaints of hunger as yet; the men were cheerful as they drank their sups of water and ate their bits of damaged bread.

It blew fresh from E.S.E. in the afternoon, and the sea began to break over the transom and quarters once more, forcing us to bail. Though choppy, the sea was flat, and old Lebogue stood on the bow thwart, shading his eyes with his hand as he gazed ahead. Suddenly he turned aft.

"Mr. Bligh!" he hailed in a subdued voice.

"Yes?"

"There's a monstrous great tortoise asleep, scarce two cable-lengths ahead! Let me conn ye on to him, sir, and I'll snatch his flipper! Many a one I've caught in the West Indies!"

Bligh nodded, with his eyes fixed on Lebogue. "Let no man make a sound," he said.

We were running at about four knots, and since the boat would almost certainly have filled had we turned broadside to the sea, there was no time to prepare a noose or to consult as to the surest method of capturing the tortoise. I knew that the slightest sound of our feet on the boat's bottom, or knock against her sides, would awaken the animal at once and send him away in alarm. Bligh was alert at the tiller, steering in accordance with the movements of Lebogue's arm. Not a word was spoken; we scarcely dared turn our heads. Once, glancing out of the corner of my eye as the stern was lifted by a breaking wave, I caught a glimpse of the broad, arched back of the sleeping tortoise, close ahead on our starboard bow. Lebogue waved to starboard a little and then raised his arm as a signal to hold the course. Next moment he stepped softly down from the thwart and leaned far over the gunwale, whilst I heard the animal's powerful thrashing in the sea. The tortoise was immensely heavy and strong, but Lebogue was a powerful man and determined not to let go. Before Smith or Lenkletter could seize his legs, — before any of us, in fact, could realize what was happening, — the tortoise had pulled him clean over the gunwale and into the sea.

A shout went up. With an oath, Mr. Bligh pushed the tiller into the master's hands and sprang to the side. "Hold me!" he shouted to Elphinstone, as he plunged his arms into the sea, straining every muscle to hold fast to Lebogue, whom he had seized by the collar of his frock. Three of us heaved the man in over the stern. He thought nothing of the wetting, but cursed his bad luck in not having captured the tortoise. Bligh praised his tenacity, and blamed the men seated near him for not holding fast to their mate.

"Had you acted promptly," he said, "instead of sitting there all agape, we should have had a feast to-night, and a supply of meat for many days! . . . Get forward, Lebogue. . . . Samuel, give him a spoonful of rum! He has earned it, by God!"

Warmed by his sup of spirit, Lebogue sat with Peckover and Cole, lamenting his lack of success, and planning what to do should another tortoise appear. "A monster," I heard him remark; "all of two hundredweight! Hold fast to my legs if we raise another —I'll never let go! Damn my eyes! To think of the grub we've lost! Did 'ee ever taste a bit of calipee?"

Bligh turned to Nelson. "Calipee!" he said, with a wry smile. "Were you ever in the West Indies, Mr. Nelson?"

"No, sir."

"I was four years in that trade, in command of Mr. Campbell's ship *Britannia*. By God, sir, those planters live like princes! When at anchor I was frequently asked to dine ashore. They used to disgust me with their stuffing and swilling of wine. Sangaree and rum punch and Madeira till one marveled they could hold it all. And the food! Pepper pot, turtle soup, turtle steaks, grilled calipee; on my word, I've seen enough, at a dinner for six, to feed us from here to Timor!"

Nelson smiled ruefully. "I could do with one of those dinners to-night," he said.

"I feel no great hunger," said Bligh, "though I would gladly have eaten a bit of raw steak."

A little before sunset the clouds broke, and we discovered land ahead — two high, rocky islands, six or eight leagues distant. The southerly island appeared of considerable extent and very high; though the light was too dazzling to see clearly, I thought it fertile and well wooded. Desiring to pass to windward of the smaller island, we hauled our wind to steer N.W. by N. At ten o'clock we were close in with the land, and could see many fires ashore. It was too dark to see more than that the island was high and rugged, and that it was inhabited; by midnight, much to our relief, we had left it astern.

We were cold and miserable during this night, and welcomed the exercise of bailing, but toward morning the wind moderated and the sea went down. At daybreak islands were in sight to the southwest, and from northwest to north, with a broad passage, not less than ten leagues wide, ahead of us. Our allowance for this day was a quarter of a pint of coconut water and two ounces of the pulp for each man. We now suffered thirst for the first time in the launch.

The islands to the southwest and northwest, be-

tween which we were steering, appeared larger than
any we had seen in this sea. Though many leagues
distant, their foreshores seemed richly wooded, and I
thought I could perceive vast plains and far-off blue
mountain ranges in the interior.

By mid-afternoon we were well between the two
great islands. The wind now moderated to a gentle
breeze from the east, and the sea became as calm
as it is within the reefs of Otaheite.

Nelson could not take his eyes off the island to the
south. "I would give five years of my life," he said
regretfully, "for an armed ship and leisure to explore
this archipelago."

"And I!" remarked the captain. "Yon island
would make ten of Otaheite! And the land to the
north seems larger still. 'Five' years! I would give
ten for a ship! No such group has yet been discovered in this sea!"

Before sunset, we were amazed, on looking over
the side, to perceive that we were sailing over a coral
bank on which there was less than a fathom of water.
Had there been the least swell to break on the shoal,
we should have been aware of it long before and sailed
clear. Since there was nothing to fear save ground-
ing, we continued on our course, keeping a sharp
lookout ahead. The launch moved slowly, through
water clear as air; I could see every detail of the
bottom. It was flat as a table, strewn with dead
coral, and barren of life, seeming to extend for about

a mile on either side of us. Twilight was giving way to dark when we came to the end of the shoal, which dropped off abruptly into deep water, as do nearly all of the coral banks in the South Sea.

A rain squall, that came on after dark, wet us to the skin and was over before we could catch more than a gallon of water. Then a cold breeze, like the night wind the people of Otaheite call *hupé*, blew down from the great valleys of the high land south of us. Though the sea was calm, we passed a wretched night, after a dinner of an ounce of damaged bread.

At daybreak our limbs were so cramped that some of the men could scarcely move. Mr. Bligh issued a teaspoonful of rum and a quarter of a pint of water, measured in his little horn cup. There was some murmuring when the morsels of damaged bread were served out. Purcell finished his bit at a single bite and a swallow, and sat shivering glumly on the thwart.

"Can't we have a bit more, sir?" Lamb begged in a low voice, of Fryer. "I'm perishin' with famine!"

"Aye!" put in Simpson. "I'd as soon be knocked on the head by cannibals as die slow the like o' this."

Bligh's quick ear caught their words. "Who's that complaining up forward?" he called. "Let them speak to me if they've anything to say."

There was an immediate silence in the bows.

"I wish to hear no more such talk," Bligh con-

tinued. "We'll share alike in this boat, and no man
shall fare better than his mates. Mind you that, all
of you!"

A fresh breeze was making up from the east. We
set the mainsail and were running at better than five
knots when they hove the log. Distant land of great
extent was now visible to the south and west, and
a small island, round and high, was discovered to the
north. The great island we had left, which bore
more the appearance of a continent than an island, was
still in sight.

We had pleasant sailing that day. The roll of
the sea from east to west seemed to be broken by the
land behind us; though the breeze filled our sails and
drove us along bravely, we shipped scarcely any water.
I exchanged places with one of the men forward, and
stationed myself in the bows, where I could watch the
flying fish rising before the launch's cutwater.

These fish were innumerable in the waters of Feejee;
I forgot my hunger, and our well-nigh hopeless situation, in the pleasure of watching them. The large
solitary kind interested me most, for it was their
custom to wait until the boat was almost upon them
before taking flight. A few powerful strokes of the
tail sent them to the surface, along which they rushed
at a great pace with the body inclined upward and
only the long lower lobe of the tail submerged. When
they had gained sufficient speed, the tail left the water
with a final strong fillip, while the fish skimmed away

through the air, steering this way and that as it pleased.

The sun was hot toward noon, and, like the others, I suffered from thirst, thinking much of the quarter of a pint of water I was soon to enjoy. As I was turning to go aft, a flying fish rose in a frenzy within ten yards, just in time to escape some large pursuer. There was a dash of spray and a blaze of gold and blue in the sea. The flying fish sped off to starboard, while a swift cleaving of the sea just beneath showed where the larger fish kept pace with its flight. It fell at last. I saw a flurry of foam, and a broad tail raised aloft for an instant.

The boatswain was on his feet. "Dolphin!" he exclaimed.

We were in the midst of a small school of them; the sea was ablaze with darting blue and gold.

Cole went aft eagerly. "I'll put a fresh bit of rag on the hook, sir," he remarked to Mr. Bligh. He began to pull in the line as he spoke, and when the hook came on board, he opened his clasp knife and cut off the bit of dingy red rag which we had hoped for so long a fish might seize.

"Try this," said the captain, taking a handkerchief of fine linen from his pocket.

We watched eagerly while the boatswain tore the handkerchief into strips and seized them on to the shank of the hook, so that the ends would trail behind in the semblance of a small mullet or cuttlefish.

When all was ready, he paid out the line, jigging the hook back and forth to attract the attention of the fish.

"Damn my eyes!" said Peckover in a low voice. "They've left us!"

"No, there they are!" I exclaimed.

A darting ripple appeared just behind the hook and sheered off. Cole pulled the line back and forth with all his art. The long dorsal fin of a dolphin clove the water like lightning behind the hook. The line straightened.

"I've got him!" roared Cole, while every man in the boat shouted at once.

The fish rushed this way and that, leaping like a salmon; but Cole's brawny arms brought him in hand-over-hand.

"Take care!" shouted Bligh; "the hook's nearly out of his mouth!"

Cole shortened his grip on the line and hove the fish aboard in one great swing. While still in the air, I saw the hook fall free; next moment the fish struck the floor of the shallow cockpit. Whilst Hallet, who sat closest, was in the act of falling on the dolphin with outstretched arms, it doubled up like a bow, gave a single powerful stroke of its tail on the floor, and flew over the gunwale and into the sea.

Tears came to Hallet's eyes. Miserably disappointed as I was, I could scarcely restrain a smile at the sight of Cole's face. Bligh gave a short, mirthless laugh. Those of the men who had risen to their feet to watch sat down in silence, and for a long time no one spoke. Cole let out his line once more, but the fish had left us, or paid no further attention to the hook.

Early in the afternoon, we hauled our wind to pass to the northward of the long, high island to the westward. It may have been one island, or many overlapping one another; in any case, it appeared of vast extent, stretching away so far to the southward that the more distant mountain ridges were lost in a bluish haze. The land was well wooded, and as we drew near I could distinguish plantations of a lighter green, regularly laid out. We were obliged to approach the land more closely than we desired, in order to pass through a channel that divided it from a small islet to the northeast.

When in the midst of this channel and no more than five miles from the land, — here distinguished by some high rocks of fantastic form, — we were alarmed to see two large canoes, sailing swiftly alongshore, and evidently in pursuit of us. They were coming on fast when the wind dropped suddenly, forcing us to take to our oars. The savages must have done the same, for they continued to gain on us for an hour or more. Then a black squall bore down from the southeast, preceded by a fierce gust of wind. It may convey some idea of the rain which fell during this squall when I say that in less than ten minutes' time, with the poor means of catching water at our disposal, we were able to replace what we had drunk from the kegs, to fill all of our empty barricos, and even the copper pot. While some of the people busied themselves with this work, others were obliged to bail to keep the water down in the bilges. The squall passed on, and a fresh breeze made up at E.S.E. We hastened to get all sail on the launch, for as the rain abated one of the canoes was perceived less than two miles from us and coming on fast. She had one mast and carried a long narrow lateen sail, something like those of the large Friendly Island vessels we had seen at Annamooka. Had the sea been rough she would have overtaken us within an hour or two, but the launch footed it fast to the northwest, with her mainsail loosed and drawing well. I felt pretty certain, from the accounts I had heard, that if captured we should probably be fattened for the slaughter, like so many geese.

As the afternoon drew on, the canoe gained on us. Most of the people kept their eyes fixed on her anxiously, but Bligh, who was at the tiller, striving to get the most out of his boat, maintained an impassive face.

"They may wish to barter," he said lightly; "yet it is better to chance no intercourse with them. If the wind holds, night will fall before they can come up with us."

Nelson scarcely took his eyes off the canoe, though

interest, and not fear, aroused him. The Indian vessel was at this time scarce a mile away.

"A double canoe," he remarked, "such as the Friendly Islanders build. See the house on the platform between. I spent a day at sea in such a vessel when I was with Captain Cook. They are manœuvred in a curious fashion; instead of tacking as we do, they wear around."

"By God!" I said earnestly. "I wish they would treat us to an exhibition of their skill!"

"How many do you reckon are on board of her?"

"Thirty or forty, I should say."

Just before sundown, when the canoe had come up to about two cable-lengths astern of us, it fell dead calm. The land at this time bore S.S.W. about eight miles distant, with a long submerged reef, on which the sea broke furiously, jutting out to the north. We were not a mile from the extremity of this reef, with a strong current setting us to the west.

"Down with the sails, lads!" Bligh commanded. "To the oars!"

There was no need to urge the men; the halyards were let go in a twinkling, and the strongest amongst us — Lebogue, Lenkletter, Cole, Purcell, Elphinstone, and the master — sprang to the oars and began to pull with all their might.

The Indians had wasted no time. Instead of paddling, as I now perceived, they sculled their vessel in a curious fashion, standing upright on the platform

between the two hulls, and plying long narrow pad-
dles not unlike our oars, which seemed to pass down
through holes in the floor. Only four men were at
these sculls, but they were frequently relieved by
others and drove the heavy double canoe, not less
than fifty feet long, quite as fast as our six could
row the launch. There was now much clamour and
shouting amongst the savages, those not sculling gazing ahead at us fiercely. One man, taller than the
others, and with an immense shock of hair, stood
on the forward end of the platform, shouting and
brandishing a great club in a kind of dance. His
gestures and the tones of his voice left no doubt as
to their intentions.

Our oarsmen pulled their best, for every man in
the boat felt pretty certain that it was a case of row
for our lives.

At the end of half an hour, Mr. Bligh perceived
that the master, a man in middle age, was weakening.
He made a sign to Peckover to relieve him, and the
gunner took the oar without missing a stroke. The
sun went down over the empty ocean on our larboard
bow, and the brief twilight of the tropics set in. The
Indians were still gaining.

Working furiously at their sculls, they were driving their vessel closer and closer to the launch. When
twilight gave place to dusk, they were not more than
a cable-length astern. The tall savage, whom I took
to be their chief, now dropped his club and strung a

bow brought forward to him. Fitting an arrow to the string, he let fly at us, and continued his practice for ten minutes or more. Some of the arrows struck the water uncomfortably close to the boat. One fell just ahead of us and floated past the side; it was nearly four feet long, made of a stiff reed, and pointed with four or five truly horrible barbs, designed to break off in the wound.

As I glanced down at this arrow, barely visible in the dusk, I heard an exclamation from Nelson, sitting next to me, and turned my head. The moon was at the full, and it was rising directly behind the Feejee canoe, throwing into relief the black figures of the savages, some sculling with furious efforts, others prancing about on her deck as they shouted like a pack of devils.

Then, for no reason we could make out, unless he acted in accordance with some superstition concerning the moon, the chief turned to shout unintelligible words to his followers. The scullers ceased their efforts and began to row slowly and steadily; the canoe bore off, turned in a wide circle, and headed back toward the land. Ten minutes later we were alone on a vast, empty, moonlit sea.

CHAPTER VI

ON the morning of May the eighth, I awoke from a
doze to find the sun half an hour high and rising in
a cloudless sky. A more blessed sight could scarcely
be imagined, for we had been drenched to the skin
the whole of the latter part of the night. Nelson,
who was beside me, was already awake, and motioned
me to silence, nodding toward Captain Bligh, who
was sleeping with his legs doubled under him on the
floor in the stern sheets, his head pillowed on one
arm, which rested on the seat. Fryer was at the
tiller, with Peckover beside him, and Cole and Lenkletter sat forward by the mast. All the others were
asleep. A gentle breeze blew; the launch was slip-
ping quietly along, and before us stretched a great
solitude of waters that seemed never to have known
a storm.

Not a word was spoken. We basked in the delicious warmth, and we could see the huddled forms
around us relax as they soaked it up in their sleep.
Captain Bligh was having his first undisturbed rest
since we had left Tofoa, and we were all desirous that
he should have the full good of it. His clothing

was as bedraggled as ours, and his cheeks were covered with a ten days' growth of beard; but although his face was pale and drawn, it lacked the expression of misery which was becoming only too apparent upon the faces of the others.

Nelson whispered to me: "Ledward, merely to look at him makes me believe in Timor." I well understood what he meant. Waking or asleep, there was that about Bligh which inspired confidence. Had we been astride a log with him, instead of in the launch, I think we might still have believed in Timor.

He slept for the better part of three hours, and, by the time he awoke, most of the others were stirring, enjoying the precious warmth of the sun, but taking good care to say nothing of our luck. Even Nelson and I were seamen enough to know that the matter should not be spoken of: that to praise good weather is to tempt it to depart. As soon as we were thoroughly warmed and had dried our clothing, we set to work cleaning the boat and stowing our possessions away in better order than we had been able to do thus far.

Captain Bligh took the occasion to provide himself with a pair of scales for weighing our food. Thus far, our daily ration had been measured by guess, but a more exact method was necessary, both to prevent the grumbling of those who thought they had received an amount smaller than their share, and also to ensure that our food should see us through.

Two or three pistol balls had been discovered under the battens in the bottom of the boat. The weight of these balls was twenty-five to the pound, and after a careful estimate of our entire amount of provisions, Bligh decided that each man's portion of bread at a meal should be equal to the weight of one ball. For scales the half shells of coconuts were used, carefully balanced against each other at the ends of a slender bar of wood to which a cord was attached, a little off the centre, as one of the coconut shells was a trifle heavier than the other. The carpenter made the scales, which served our purpose admirably, but it was a woeful sight to all to see how little of the bread was needed to balance the musket ball. Our allowance of food was now fixed at one twenty-fifth of a pound of bread and a quarter of a pint of water per man, to be served at eight in the morning, at noon, and at sunset. What remained of the salt pork was saved for occasions when we should be in need of a more substantial repast. We still had several coconuts, and, while they lasted, used the meat of these in place of bread, and the liquid in the nuts instead of water; but, as I remember it, we ate the last of them on the tenth of May.

The method of serving our food was this: A portion of bread, of an amount about sufficient for the company, was taken from the chest and handed back in a cloth to Captain Bligh, who usually weighed out the eighteen rations, and they were then passed along from hand to hand. The water, which was stored amidships, was measured, usually by Fryer or Nelson or myself, while Mr. Bligh was weighing the bread, the cup used being a small horn drinking-vessel; and the water was then poured into one of the wineglasses, and handed to the men as they received their bread. It was curious to see the manner in which they accepted and dispatched their food. It was "dispatch" indeed, with most of them; their meal would be finished in an instant.

Purcell was among this number. No matter how miserable I might be, I found relief in watching him receive his tiny morsel. It was always with the same expression of amazement and injury. He would hold the bread in the palm of his huge hand for a few seconds, peering at it from under his shaggy eyebrows as though not quite certain it was there. Then he would clap it into his mouth with an expression of disgust still more comical, and roll up his eyes as though asking heaven to witness that he had not received his due allowance.

Some followed Mr. Bligh's example. He soaked his bread in a coconut shell, in his allowance of water, and then ate it very slowly so that he had the illusion, at least, of having enjoyed a meal.

Samuel, Bligh's clerk, followed a practice that did, in fact, provide him with what might be called the ghost of a meal. With the exception of his breakfast allowance of water, he would save his food and drink until the evening, when he had it all at once. This was, of course, a legitimate privilege, but I think Samuel's reason for exercising it was that he wished to gloat over his food while some of his near companions look hungrily on. I must give him credit for his self-restraint; but in Samuel it did not, somehow, appear to advantage. I can still hear old Purcell's exasperated voice: "Damn your eyes, Samuel! Don't lick your chops over it! Eat and be done with it like the rest of us!"

Cole never failed to say grace before he partook of his food, however tiny the amount. His little prayer, delivered in a low voice, was audible to those who sat next him in the boat. I heard it, many's the time; and it was always the same: "Our Heavenly Father: We thank Thee for Thy ever-loving care, and for these Thy bounties to the children of men."

One might easily have imagined, from the simple, earnest manner of the old fellow, that he had just sat down to a table spread with all the good things of life, and that he considered such largess far beyond his deserts.

The afternoon continued fine, with the same gentle breeze carrying us smoothly in the direction we would go. At midday Bligh took our position. By our log we had sailed sixty-two miles since noon of the seventh, the smallest day's run we had yet made; but we were content that it should be so, for we had comfort from the sun's warmth and rest from the weary work of bailing.

We had sailed five hundred miles from Tofoa, nearly one-seventh of the distance to Timor; an average better than eighty miles per day. That number, somehow, encouraged us; we made much of it, passed it about in talk. Five hundred miles seemed a vast distance; but we were careful to avoid speaking of the more than three thousand miles that lay ahead.

On this day Mr. Bligh performed an act of heroism in having himself shaved by Smith, his servant. There was neither soap nor water to soften his beard. He sat on the floor in the stern sheets, his head held between Peckover's knees, while Smith crouched beside him cutting through the dry hair, stopping every moment to strop his razor. The task required the better part of an hour; and none of us, seeing Bligh's sufferings, was tempted to follow his example.

"By God, Smith!" he said when the ordeal was over. "I would run the gantlet of all the savages in the South Sea rather than go through this again. Were you ever shaved by the Indians, Mr. Nelson?"

"Once," Nelson replied. "Captain Cook and I both made the experiment on the island of Leefooga. The native made use of two shells, taking the hairs of the beard between them. It was a tedious task, but not so painful as I had imagined it would be."

Bligh nodded. "I've tried it myself; and I've

heard that an Indian mother can shave her child's
head with a shark's tooth on a stick, and make as close
work of it as a man could do with a razor. But I'll
believe that only when I've seen it done."

"They've great skill, the Indians," said Peckover;
"but my choice is for our own way. I'd be pleased
to be sitting this minute in the chair of the worst hair-
dresser in Portsmouth. I'd call it heaven, though
he shaved me with a wood rasp."

"You'll see Portsmouth again, Mr. Peckover; never
doubt it," said Bligh quietly.

A deep silence followed this statement. The men
looked toward him, a pathetic, wistful eagerness apparent on every face. All wished to believe; and yet
the chances against us seemed overwhelming. But
there was no shadow of uncertainty in Bligh's voice
or manner. He spoke with a confidence that cheered
us all.

"And another thing we will see there," he went on:
"Fletcher Christian hanging by the neck from a
yardarm on one of His Majesty's ships, and every
bloody pirate that joined him."

"It will be a long day, Mr. Bligh, before we have
that satisfaction, if we ever do," Purcell replied.

"Long?" Bligh replied. "The arm of His Majesty's
law is long, mind you that! Let them hide as they
may, it can reach and take them by the neck. Mr.
Nelson, where do you think they will go? I have
my own opinion, but I should like yours."

This was the first time since we had lost the ship that Mr. Bligh had made more than a passing blasphemous reference to the mutineers, or would suffer any of us to speak of them.

"I can tell you where I think most of them will wish to go," Nelson replied: "back to Otaheite."

"So I think," said Bligh. "May God make them bloody fools enough to do it!"

"As they cast off the launch, sir, I plainly heard some of them shout 'Huzza for Otaheite!'" Elphinstone put in. "There was much noise at the time, but I couldn't have been mistaken."

"Whatever the others may decide to do," said Nelson, "there is one too wise to stop there long: Mr. Christian."

Bligh started as though he had been struck in the face. He glanced darkly at Nelson, his eyes blazing with suppressed anger.

"Mr. Nelson," he said; "let me never again hear a title of courtesy attached to that scoundrel's name!"

"I am sorry," Nelson replied quietly.

"Say no more," said Bligh. "It was a slip, that I know; but I could not suffer it to pass in silence. . . . I agree with what you say of him. He is too wily a villain to remain in a place where he knows he will be searched for. But you will see: the others will not follow him; and we shall have them, like that!" He opened his hand, closing it slowly and tightly as though he already had their several throats within his clutch.

"Aye," said Purcell sourly. "And the leader of 'em will go free. He'll never be found."

"Say you so?" Bligh replied with a harsh laugh. "You should know me better than that, Mr. Purcell. I pray I may be sent in search of him! There's not an island in the Pacific, charted or not, where he can escape me! No, by God! Not a sandy cay in the midst of desolation where I cannot track him down! And well he knows it!"

"Where do you think he might go, sir?" asked Fryer.

"We will speak no more of this matter, Mr. Fryer," Bligh replied, and there was an end to any discussion of the mutineers for many a day. Bligh felt keenly the humiliation of losing his ship, and although he rarely mentioned the *Bounty*, well we knew that the thought of her was always present in his mind.

That same afternoon he gave us an account of what he knew of the coastal lands of New Holland and New Guinea.

"This information is for you in particular, Mr. Fryer, and for Mr. Elphinstone," he said. "Should anything happen to me it will devolve upon you to navigate those waters, and you must know what I can tell you of the course to follow. That ocean is but little known; my knowledge of it I had from Captain Cook, when I was master of the *Resolution*, on his third voyage. Our task then was largely concerned with exploration in the Northern Hemisphere; but we had much time on our hands at sea, and Captain Cook was kind enough to inform his officers of his earlier explorations in the western Pacific, and of his passage through what he named 'Endeavour Straits.' I listened with interest, but I little thought I should ever have use for the information he gave us. Which only goes to show, young man," he added, turning to Hayward, "that knowledge of the sea never comes amiss to a seaman. Remember that. You never know when you may have occasion to use it."

"Is there any other passage between those lands save by Endeavour Straits?" Elphinstone asked.

"There may be," Bligh replied; "but if so, I've never heard of it. I need not go into the details of my recollection of the position as given by Captain Cook. You will find this marked on the rough chart I made from memory whilst we were in the cave at Tofoa. It is in my journal. That chart is all you will have to go by in steering through what Captain Cook considered the worst area of reef-infested ocean in the whole of the Pacific. This is the important thing to bear in mind now: Whether we will or no, with strong winds and a heavy sea we must run before them, very likely, farther to the north than we wish to go. Therefore, in case you are driven north of the twelfth parallel, take every opportunity to get to the south'ard, so that you may strike the great reef

along the coast of New Holland in the region of
thirteen south.   It is thereabout, as I recall it, that
Captain Cook found the passage which he named
'Providential Channel.'   If you can strike it, you can
coast to the north'ard with a fair wind, in tolerably
quiet waters, till you round the northern cape of New
Holland and pass through Endeavour Straits.   You
shall then have open sailing all the way to Timor."

"We shan't forget, sir," Fryer replied; "but God
forbid that you should not be the one to see us
through!"

"God will forbid it, I believe," said Bligh, gravely;
"but in our situation it is best to provide for every
possible mishap."

"Will there be islands, sir, inside the reef at New
Holland, where we can go ashore?" Hayward asked.

"I have a clear recollection of Captain Cook speaking of various small lands scattered over the lagoons,"
Bligh replied.   "He found none that were inhabited,
as I remember, although he believed they were resorted to at times by the savages.   We shall certainly
stop at some of them to refresh ourselves."

"How far will New Holland be from where we
are, sir?" Hallet asked.

"We will not speak of that, my lad," said Bligh in
a kindly voice.   "Think if you like of the distance we
have come, but never let your mind run forward
faster than your vessel.   Lebogue is an old seaman.
Ask him if that is good advice."

"Aye, sir, the very best," said Lebogue, nodding his shaggy head. "It's the only way for a quick passage, Mr. Hallet."

We fell silent again, watching Lebogue, who sat at our solitary fishing line, which he had kept in the water nearly all the way from Tofoa. We had no bait to spare, and Lebogue and the boatswain had tried every conceivable kind of lure that our means afforded. He was now using one made of the brass handle of a clasp knife and some bits of red cloth torn from a handkerchief. It trailed after the launch at a distance of forty or fifty yards, and was sometimes drawn closer that we might better observe it. There had been moments of breathless expectation when some fish of splendid size would rush toward it; but they invariably recognized it as belonging to nothing in nature, and sheered away. It was maddening to see fish around us—often great multitudes—and never to be able to catch one. But Cole and Lebogue were ever hopeful. They were continually changing the lure; but the result was always the same. On several occasions schools of small mulletlike fish had hovered alongside of us for a few moments. Had we been possessed of a hoop net we could, unquestionably, have caught some of them, they were in such quantities, but the attempt to seine them up with our few remaining hats had not been successful. For all our bitter disappointments, both the fish and the occasional sea birds we met with proved a boon to us. Attempts to catch them occupied our minds. Our bellies, however, felt differently about the matter, and would never agree that our unavailing attempts did more than add insult to injury.

We now had both sails up; they were drawing well, and the sea was so calm that we shipped no water. The sun went down, as it had risen, in a cloudless sky, and darkness came on swiftly. Presently the moon rose, flooding the lonely sea with a glory that transfigured our little boat and everyone in her. Purcell, with his dirty rags wound round his broken head, sat by the mast amidships, facing aft. He looked a noble, even an heroic figure, in that light. On the day of the mutiny, as we were rowing away from the *Bounty*, I wondered how long one small boat would hold two such men as Captain Bligh and himself before they would be at each other's throats. There had long been a feud between them on the ship. Purcell had a high opinion of his ability as a carpenter, and considered himself a monarch in his own department. He was as bullheaded as Bligh himself, but he had the good sense to know his place and to realize that the captain of a ship was, after all, in a position of higher authority than the carpenter. Secretly, as I knew, he gloried in the fact that Bligh had lost his ship, and considered it a just punishment for his tyrannical behaviour; and yet there was no man more loyal to his commander. On the morning of the mutiny there had not been a moment's hesitation in deciding where his duty lay. In the launch it interested me to observe his attitude toward Bligh, and Bligh's toward him. They hated each other; but, in Purcell's case at least, hatred was tempered by respect.

What a contrast the carpenter made to young Tinkler, who sat beside him! He loved this lad as much as he hated Bligh, and being an old seaman he invariably showed him great respect because of his rank as midshipman, never omitting to address him as "Mr. Tinkler." And Tinkler was worthy of respect as well as of affection. He was a plucky lad. There was never a time, no matter how desperate our situation, when he did not play his part like a man.

That night was the only one we had passed in any measure of comfort since leaving Tofoa. Our cramped positions were no pleasanter than they had been, but the boat, as well as our cloathing, was dry, and we were able to have some hours of refreshing sleep.

The ninth of May was just such a day as the eighth had been, with a calm sea and a light breeze from the east-southeast. Bligh had everyone roused at dawn, and as soon as we had worked a little of the stiffness out of our limbs, he set Cole to work, with some of us for helpers, in fitting a pair of shrouds for each mast. Others assisted the carpenter, who was employed in putting a weather cloth, made of some of our spare canvas, around the boat. The quarters were raised nine inches by means of the stern seats which were

nailed to cleats along them, and the weather cloth
was of the same width, so that, when the task was
finished, the boat was as well prepared for rough
weather as we could make her.   This was the carpenter's day, and he made the most of it; and I will do
him the justice to say that he did a thoroughly work-
manlike job.

I was glad to hear Mr. Bligh remark: "That will do
very well, carpenter."

It was high praise, coming from him; but Purcell
would not have been Purcell had he not replied:
"Begging your pardon, sir, it won't do well, but I can
make no better with what we've got here."

At noon, on the ninth, we were sixty-four miles
farther on our way.   All of this day we saw neither
fish nor bird.

Toward the middle of the afternoon, Nelson broke
a silence that seemed to have lasted for hours.   "I am
constrained to speak, Mr. Bligh," he said, with a faint
smile.   "This sea is so vast and so quiet that I am inclined to doubt its reality and our own as well."

"That's a strange fancy, sir," Bligh replied; "but
the sea is real enough; I can promise you that."

CHAPTER VII

I REMEMBER Captain Bligh saying to Fryer, about noon on May the twelfth: "I think we've seen the worst of it."

"I am sure of it, sir," Fryer replied, but he believed no more than Bligh in the truth of the statement. It had fallen calm about half an hour before, but the sea, as viewed from the launch, was an awe-inspiring sight. Fryer had just relieved Bligh at the tiller, which he had held continuously for eighteen hours.

Our shrouds for the masts and the canvas weather cloth had been fitted none too soon; on the evening of that same day,—May the ninth,—at about nine o'clock, wind and rain had struck us together, and all through the night four men were continuously bailing, and there were times when every man of us save Bligh was so employed. The sky was concealed by low gray clouds scudding before the wind. So it remained all day and all night of the tenth, the eleventh, and till near midday of the twelfth; and now, although the wind had fallen, the sky was an ominous sight.

There was no break in the clouds, no signs of a

lightening at any point in the heavy canopy that overhung us, so low that it seemed almost within reach. Nevertheless, it was calm, for the moment, at least, and the sky withheld its rain. Our sail was dropped into the boat.

"I want two men at the oars," Bligh said.

"I'll make one, sir," Lenkletter called out, and a dozen others at the same time. All were eager for a chance to warm their benumbed bodies. Lenkletter and Lebogue were first chosen, but there were reliefs every quarter of an hour so that the rest of us might enjoy the benefit of the exercise.

"Don't exert yourselves, men," said Bligh; "merely keep her stern to the swell."

The boat had never seemed so small to me as she did then, and I could imagine what a speck she would have appeared in that vast ocean could one have observed her with a sea bird's eye. The long swell, coming from the southeast, was of a prodigious height, but without the wind there was no menace in it. The seas moved toward us, rank after rank, with a solemnity, a majesty, that filled the heart with awe; cold and wretched though we were, we had a kind of solemn pleasure in watching them: seeing our little boat lifted high on their broad backs, to find ourselves immediately after in a great valley between them.

As a recompense for our sufferings, Captain Bligh issued an allowance of rum, two teaspoonfuls for each man; and for our dinner that day we had half an ounce of pork each, in addition to the bread. This made our midday meal seem a veritable feast, and the rum gave us a little warmth. It was the cold that we dreaded at this time, fully as much as the sea: the wind, penetrating cloathing perpetually drenched with rain, felt bitterly chill, as though it were blowing from fields of ice. Thanks to Captain Bligh, we now adopted a means of combating it that proved of inestimable service. He advised us to wring out our cloathing in sea water. It is strange that none of us had thought of this simple expedient before, but the fact remains that we had not. The moment we tried it we found ourselves wonderfully comfortable in comparison with our miserable plight before, the reason being that salt water does not evaporate in the wind so fast as fresh.

We passed the next two or three hours tolerably well; what between taking our turns at the oars and wringing out our cloathes from time to time, we broke the back of the afternoon, each man secretly watching all the while for any change that would give us reason to hope that better weather was in store; but the only change was that the dull light became duller yet, as the day wore on toward evening. And still there was no wind.

The silence made us uneasy. Our ears had been accustomed to the deep roar of the wind and the seething hiss of breaking seas. God knows, we wanted no more of such weather, but we did crave wind enough to carry us on our way. The great swells went under us noiselessly; the only sounds to be heard were the small human sounds within the boat — a spoken word, a cough, a weary sigh as someone shifted his position.

It must have been toward four o'clock in the afternoon that there was mingled with the vast quiet what was, at first, the very ghost of sound — and yet every man of us heard it. Elphinstone, who was lying in the bottom of the boat just before me, raised his head to look round. "What is that?" he said.

There was no need to reply. As we rose to the swell, every head was turned to the eastward; and there, not half a mile distant, we again saw approaching our remorseless enemy — rain.

It came on in what appeared to be a solid wall of blackness, faintly lighted by a dull grayish glow from the sky before it. There was no wind immediately behind; the slowness of its approach assured us of that; therefore, we waited in silence, while the sound increased and spread, now deadened as we fell into the trough, more loud as we rose to the crest of the next wave. Then, as though at the last moment it had leaped to make sure of us, we were in the midst of it — drenched, half drowned, gasping for breath, in a deluge such as we had never before experienced.

In an instant I lost sight of the men in the forward part of the boat. This, I know, will scarcely be believed by those whose experience of rain has been only

in the northern latitudes, who know nothing of the
enormous weight of water released in a tropical cloud-
burst. The fact remains that the launch vanished
from my sight save for the after part of it where I
sat, and the men immediately before my eyes were but
shadows blurred by sheets of almost solid water. I
heard Captain Bligh's voice, faintly, above the hiss
and thunder of the deluge. The words were indis-
tinguishable, but we well knew what we had to do.
We bailed with the desperation of men who feel the
water gaining upon them even as they bail; who feel
it cover their feet and rise slowly toward their knees.
And it was not sea water that we threw over the side.
It was the pure sweet water of clouds, which men,
adrift in a small boat in mid-ocean, so often pray for
in vain, with blackening lips and swelling tongues;
and we hurled it away from us with bailing scoops,
coconut shells, the copper pot, with our hats, with our
cupped hands, lest this precious fluid, which Captain
Bligh had, rightly, doled out to us a quarter of a pint
at a time, should be our death. There was irony in
the situation, though we had no time to think of it
then.

The darkness in the midst of the storm was almost
that of night, but presently I could once more see
the outlines of the boat and the forms of the men, and
knew that the worst was over. We were a forlorn-
looking crew: the water streamed from our cloathing,
which was plastered against our bodies; from our hair
and beards; and we were again chilled to the bone.

Mr. Bligh's voice sounded unusually loud against the ensuing silence. "Look alive, lads! Mr. Cole, close-reef the foresail, and get it on her. There'll be wind behind this."

"Aye, aye, sir," the boatswain called back. The rest of us, with the exception of the men at the oars, continued bailing, for there was a deal of water yet to be got rid of.

Lebogue was working beside me. "Aye," he muttered, at Bligh's remark about wind; "we've summ'at to come, I'll be bound."

We bailed her dry, and then had time, for a few moments, to know how cold we were. "Wring out your cloathes," said Bligh. We were not slow to obey, and the men nearest Lamb and Simpson performed this service for them, as they were too weak to do it for themselves. Meanwhile the foresail had been double-reefed and hoisted, Bligh again took the tiller, and we waited for the wind.

We saw it coming from afar. The oily swells, that had been smooth enough to reflect the gray light, were blackened under it. We saw it leaping from summit to summit; but whilst it came swiftly, there was no great weight of air at first. Our tiny bit of sail, heavy and dark with rain, bellied out, and the launch gathered steerageway once more. The dull light faded from the sky, and soon what was left of it seemed to be gathered on the surface of the sea, again streaked with foam and flying spray. Harder and harder it blew. No watch was set for the night.

We well knew there was work and to spare at hand for all of us.

Nelson touched my arm and pointed overhead. A man-of-war bird, its great wings outspread, wheeled into the wind and hovered over us for a few seconds, seeming to stand motionless against that mighty stream as it looked down at us. Of a sudden it tipped, scudded away, and was lost to view.

Fryer was seated by Mr. Bligh, watching the following seas. "Stand by to bail!" he shouted.

I cannot recall the thirty-six hours that followed without experiencing something of the horror I felt at the time. Wind and rain, rain and wind, under a sky that held no promise of relief. Bad as the hours of daylight were, those of darkness were infinitely worse, for we could see nothing. It seemed a miracle to me that Mr. Bligh was able to keep the launch before the seas, the more so because the wind veered considerably at times, and he could not depend upon the feel of it at his back to tell him how the waves were approaching. He was helped to some extent by Fryer and Elphinstone, who crouched on their knees beside him, facing aft, peering into the darkness; but with the clouds of spray continually in their faces, they could see little or nothing until a sea was on the point of boarding us.

Never, I think, could the gray dawn have been welcomed more devoutly than it was by us on the morning of May the fourteenth; and, as though in pity of our plight, the wind abated shortly after. There was even a watery gleam of light as the sun rose, but our hopes and prayers for blue sky were unavailing. Nevertheless, the clouds were higher and the look of them less menacing than they had been for four days past.

As I looked into the faces about me I realized how frightful my own must appear. Lamb, the butcher, and George Simpson, the quartermaster's mate, appeared to be at the last extremity. They lay in the bottom of the boat, unable to do aught for themselves; throughout the night just past, the water we shipped continually had been washing around them, and it was as much as they could do at times to raise their heads above it. Nelson, too, was a pitiable sight. Never a strong man, the privations and hardships we had undergone had worn him down, but the spirit within the frail body was as tough as that of Captain Bligh himself. Never a groan or a word of complaint came from Nelson. Weak as he was, physically, he was a tower of strength in our company. The men who showed the fewest signs of suffering thus far were Purcell, Cole, Peckover, Lenkletter, Elphinstone, and the three midshipmen. Captain Bligh and the master, who had borne the brunt of our battle against the sea, were gaunt and hollow-eyed, but Bligh seemed to have an inexhaustible reserve of energy to draw upon. I must not omit to speak of Samuel, Bligh's clerk, whom I had thought would be among the first to show the effects of hardship. He was city born and bred, with the pale complexion and the soft-appearing body usually found among men of sedentary occupations; nevertheless, he had borne up amazingly well, both in body and spirit. He was a man wholly lacking in imagination, and his belief in Captain Bligh was like that of a dog for its master. He would not, I am sure, conceive of any situation, however perilous, which Bligh was not more than equal to. I envied him this confident trust, particularly at night. Tinkler and Hayward were sturdily built lads, and youth gave them a great advantage over some of the rest of us. Hallet lacked their toughness of fibre, but for all that he played his part like a man, and deserved the more credit in that he was compelled to fight constantly against his terror of the sea. He was not the only one with this fear at his heart. I admit freely that my spirits were often far sunk because of it, although I did my best to conceal the fact.

There had been times, at night, when no man of us, unless it were Samuel,—no, not even Captain Bligh himself,—could have believed that we should see another dawn. The fact that we had survived the nights of the thirteenth and fourteenth gave us new courage. We knew, now, what our boat could do.

We were on a course, N.W. by W. Of a sudden

the gray sky to the southwest lightened, and a few
moments later there was a break in the clouds. We
had all around us, as we thought, nothing but empty
sea; but presently we saw, or thought we saw, pale-
blue mountains that seemed to be floating high in air.
Tinkler was the first to spy them, and before some of
us could raise our heads to look, they had again vanished in the mists. Those who had not seen could not
believe in the reality of the vision, but an hour later,
there it was again; and this time there was no doubt
in anyone's mind. Clouds of dense vapour lifted
slowly, revealing a land of lofty mountains that stood
in cold blue silhouette against the gray sky. At first
we thought it one island; but as we approached we
found there were four, which bore S.W. to N.W. by
W., and distant about six leagues. The largest was,
in Captain Bligh's judgment, about twenty leagues
in circuit.

We altered our course to pass a little to the eastward of the most northerly one. Bligh had only
his recollection to serve him, but he believed them a
part of the New Hebrides, which Captain Cook had
named and explored during his second expedition to
the South Sea, in 1774. All through the morning we
were sailing at about two knots. The sea was now so
calm that but two men were required at the bailing
scoops. The rest of us feasted our eyes upon the land.
Many an anxious and appealing glance was thrown
in Captain Bligh's direction, but he gave no hint as

to what his plan was. By the middle of the afternoon we had left the larger islands well astern, and
were no more than two leagues distant from the
northerly one. The wind was again blowing fresh,
and our course was altered to approach still closer.
We could see the smoke of many fires rising from the
foreshore; the thought of their warmth increased our
misery.

The land was of a horseshoe shape. A ridge of high
mountains, falling steeply to the sea, enclosed a large
bay with a northeasterly exposure. We passed the
entrance to this bay not more than two miles off. In
about half an hour we had rounded the northern cape,
and were well in the lee.

No word had been spoken during this time. We
waited with deep anxiety to learn what Captain
Bligh's intentions were.

"Trim the sails," he ordered.

We headed up, approaching to within a quarter of
a mile of a small cove that resembled, in a general
way, the one at Tofoa; but here there was a smooth
sandy beach instead of a rocky one, and the vegetation
was of the richest green; indeed, the island seemed a
paradise to our famished, sea-weary eyes. The sail
was dropped and two men were set at the oars to keep
us off the land.

"Now, Mr. Purcell," said Bligh, "we will repair
our weather cloth. Look alive, for I wish to lose no
more time here than is necessary."

Our weather cloth had been much damaged by the sea the night before.

A deep silence followed this order. Purcell remained where he was. Presently he raised his head, sullenly.

"Mr. Bligh," he said, "if you mean to go on from here without giving us a chance to refresh ourselves, I'm opposed; and there's more that feels as I do."

For all the stiffness in his legs, Bligh got to his feet in an instant. His lips were drawn in a thin line and his eyes were blazing with anger, but as he looked at the forlorn figures before him the expression on his face softened and he checked himself.

"There are more?" he asked quietly. "Who are they? Let them speak up."

"I'm one, sir," Elphinstone replied in a hollow voice; "and I'll ask you to believe I'm speaking for others more than myself."

"We are in a pitiful state, sir," Fryer put in. "A night of rest on shore might be the means of preserving the lives of some of us. There's sure to be food on so rich an island."

"There's coconut trees, sir," Lenkletter put in eagerly. "Look yonder, halfway up the slope."

A clump of coconut palms could, in fact, be seen, raising their plumed tops above the forests that covered the steep hillsides. Bligh looked from us to the land, and back again; presently he shook his head.

"Lads, we dare not risk it," he said. "You cannot

suppose that I do not feel for your sufferings, since
I share them with you. God knows I should be glad
to rest here; but the danger is too great. We must
not!"

"There's no Indians here, sir," said Purcell.
"That's plain to be seen."

Bligh controlled himself with difficulty. "At the
moment there are none," he replied; "but we have
seen the smoke of many fires, and we were well within
view as we passed the bay on the northern side. Make
no mistake, we have been seen; and I will say this,
which may cool your desire to go ashore: Captain
Cook told me that the savages of the New Hebrides
are cannibals of the fiercest sort. These islands must
be a part of the same group."

"I don't fear them," Purcell interrupted, "whatever may be the case with yourself."

Bligh jerked back his head, as though he had been
struck in the face. Purcell, always a cantankerous
old rogue, had never before dared to speak in this
fashion. Some allowance, perhaps, can be made for
him under the circumstances. Although he had
borne hardships well, it is possible that he felt the
pangs of hunger more keenly than any of us.

Mr. Bligh behaved with a forbearance I had
thought him incapable of exercising. Frequently, on
the *Bounty*, I had seen him fly into a passion upon
slight provocation. Now that he had ample cause
for anger, he kept himself well in hand. The reason

was, I believe, that he knew how desperately weary we were and how bitter our disappointment at being within view of what appeared to us Eden itself, and forbidden to rest and refresh ourselves there. No insult could have been more gross and unjust than that of the carpenter, and he well knew it.

For a moment Bligh did not trust himself to speak. Then he said: "Set about your work, Mr. Purcell. If you do not, by God you *shall* go ashore — with me, and with me alone."

The carpenter, knowing that he was in the wrong, obeyed at once. Those who had the strength assisted him; the rest of us kept watch on shore.

Presently Lebogue exclaimed: "Aye, sir, we've been seen, right enough! Look yonder!"

Half a dozen savages emerged from the thick bush and came down to the water's edge, gazing out toward us. We were directly opposite the entrance to the cove, and could see them plainly. They were naked save for short kirtles about the middle, and were armed with spears, bows, and arrows. About this same time, Tinkler and Hayward discovered a path leading up one of the hills at the beck of the cove. At one point it was in plain view, where it rounded a grassy knoll. Keeping watch upon this place, we saw more Indians passing it as they hastened into the valley. The beach was soon thronged, and we could faintly hear their shouts as they ran this way and that, evidently in a state of great excitement. We had the entire half circle of the beach within view; no canoes were to be seen there, but we did not know what they might have concealed amongst the trees.

In view of Purcell's bold statement of half an hour before, it was interesting to observe his nervousness as the throng of savages increased. Many an apprehensive glance did he throw in their direction.

"Keep your eyes on your work, sir!" Bligh ordered. "Your friends ashore will wait for you."

Presently Tinkler, who had the keenest eyes amongst us, informed Bligh that he had seen three or four of the Indians running up the hill, evidently returning to the large bay on the other side of the mountains.

"They must be sending word to the people over there, sir," Fryer remarked, anxiously. "No doubt they have canoes in the bay, and mean to get at us by sea."

"I should think it more than likely, sir," Bligh replied, quietly. "Nevertheless, we shall have time to finish repairing our weather cloth."

Never, I fancy, had Purcell worked more earnestly than he did upon this occasion. Bligh watched him grimly and would allow him to skimp nothing.

Just as the work was finished, a large canoe, containing between forty and fifty savages, appeared round the northern promontory, about a mile distant. They had no sail, but, with ten or fifteen paddlers on a side, they came on swiftly.

"Now, Mr. Purcell," said Bligh; "is it your desire that we let them come up with us? You say you have no fear of them."

It was all but impossible for the carpenter ever to admit himself in the wrong; but upon this occasion he swallowed his stubborn pride at once.

"No, sir," he replied.

"Very well," said Bligh. "Get sail on her, Mr. Cole."

For all the stiffness of our limbs, the two sails were hoisted in an instant, and we drew away from the land. For the moment, at least, we forgot our hunger, our wet cloathing—everything was lost sight of in the excitement of the race. At first the savages gained rapidly, and it was plain from their actions that their intentions were anything but friendly: those who were not paddling brandished their weapons, and several of them shot arrows after us, some of which fell only a little distance astern. Then we caught the full force of the wind, and the space between us gradually increased. Presently they gave up the pursuit; we saw them enter the cove opposite which we had lain. We then stood away upon the old course.

Never, I think, during the whole of our voyage, were our spirits so low as upon this same afternoon. The sea stretched away, gray and solitary, and we dared not think of the horizons beyond horizons that remained to be crossed before we could set foot upon any shore. Most of us knew that we were still far from halfway, even, to the coast of New Holland. At the earliest we could not hope to reach it before another fortnight had passed.

I now come to an incident concerning which I am most reluctant to speak, and yet it must not be passed over in silence. There was, it seems, one man in our company so lost to all sense of his duty toward the others as to steal a part of our precious supply of pork. The theft amounted to one two-pound piece, and was committed during the night of this same day. With respect to the bread, Captain Bligh had put temptation beyond the power of anyone: it was kept under lock and key in the carpenter's chest. But the pork was not so guarded. It was stored, wrapped in a cloth, in the bow. We had passed a wretched night, with a strong northeast wind, a rough sea, and perpetual rain. There had been no sleep for anyone. At dawn the next morning, Captain Bligh ordered a teaspoonful of rum and half an ounce of pork for our breakfast; and it was then that the theft was discovered. I well remember the look of horror in Mr. Cole's face as he reported it. "There's a piece missing, sir," he said.

I should not have supposed that any man guilty of such a crime against his comrades could have maintained an air of perfect innocence upon the discovery of the theft; but so it was, here. Captain Bligh questioned each of us by name, beginning with the master: —

"Mr. Fryer, did you take this pork?"

"No, sir," Fryer replied, with a sincerity that no one could doubt.

The question was repeated seventeen times, and the seventeen replies all carried conviction.

I remember having heard, or read, that men reduced to starvation in company sometimes lose all sense of moral responsibility, and that cases have been known where men of integrity, under normal conditions, have committed such crimes without any qualms of conscience, stoutly and indignantly denying them, no matter how damning the evidence against them might be. With us there was no evidence as to the possible culprit; most of our company had taken turns at bailing in the bow during the night, which was so black that one could not see one's next neighbour in the boat.

I shall say no more of this wretched affair except that the thief, whoever he may have been, must surely have despised himself. Captain Bligh brought home to him the enormity of the wrong he had done his fellow sufferers in words that he can never forget.

I believed, on the night of the fourteenth of May, that our company had suffered to the limits of endurance. "Another night as bad as this . . ." I had thought. And there were to be nine to follow —nine days and nights, during which time we were continuously wet and all but perished with cold. The wind shifted from southeast to northeast, now blowing half a gale, now dying away to a dead calm when the oars would be gotten out to keep the launch before the sea. There were moments of fugitive sunshine, but of such brief duration that they but added to our misery, for we were never able to dry our cloathes.

Our situation on the afternoon of May twenty-third was so like that of the twelfth that it seemed time had stood still. We rode the same mountainous seas, under the same lowering sky. What added to my confused sense that we were doomed to an eternity of misery was that Mr. Bligh had again remarked to Fryer: "I think we've seen the worst of it."

We had been on starvation rations for twenty-one days past, and, during the whole of this time, wet to the skin and chilled to the bone. Our bodies were covered with salt-water sores, so that the slightest movement was agony, yet we were compelled to move constantly for the purpose of bailing. Many of us were now too weak to raise ourselves to our feet, but we crawled and pulled ourselves about somehow, and, knowing that our lives depended upon it, we could still manage to throw out water.

Never before had I realized what a torment the body could be. But I must add this: neither had I realized the toughness, the fineness, of the human spirit under conditions that try it to the utmost. The miscreant who had stolen the pork served only as a foil to the others, whose conduct was such during these interminable hours of trial as has given me a new and exalted opinion of my fellow beings. Whatever men may say in men's despite in the future, or whatever unfortunate revelations concerning them may come under my own observation, I shall think of the company in the *Bounty's* launch and retain my firm belief that, in their darkest hours, and in situations that bear upon them even past the limits of endurance, most men show a heroism that lifts them to heights beyond estimation. The cynic may smile at this. I care not. I know whereof I speak. I have seen the matter put to the proof in a company of eighteen whose members, with two exceptions, — Captain Bligh and Mr. Nelson, — were men such as one might find in any seacoast town in England.

I will not say that there had been no complaints, no urgent, piteous requests for additional food. There were. I can understand better now than I could then what strength Bligh needed to withstand the entreaties of starving men. He fed the weakest upon wine, a few drops at a time; but every demand for additional food was refused save upon the occasions when a tiny morsel of pork would be added to our mouthful of bread.

I have a vivid recollection of the events of the evening and the night of May twenty-third. Bligh had been continuously at the tiller for thirty-six hours, and he remained there until dawn the following morning. I sat in the bottom of the boat facing him, propped up against the thwart immediately forward of the stern sheets. Nelson lay beside me with his head on my knee. He was frightfully emaciated, and so weak that I believed he had not more than twenty-four hours to live. The strongest of our number were Mr. Bligh, Fryer, Cole, Peckover, Samuel, and the two midshipmen, Tinkler and Hayward. The two latter were at the oars as the last of daylight faded, keeping the launch before the sea.

It had been dead calm for more than two hours, but neither past experience nor the look of the sky gave us reason to expect that it would remain so. The last gray light faded quickly, and soon we were in the complete darkness that had been our portion during so many terrible nights.

About three hours after sunset I had fallen into a doze, and only a moment later, it seemed, I was awakened by the deep humming of the wind and the hiss and wash of breaking seas. I heard Bligh calling to Cole, whose station was forward by the reefed foresail, and immediately afterward solid water came pouring over our quarters. Never had we come so near to foundering as at that moment; indeed, for a few seconds I thought we were lost. Bligh shouted: "Bail for your lives!" and so we did. Not a man of us but realized that we were in the immediate presence of disaster.

The horror of that experience I shall not attempt

to describe; but it had this good effect: that it aroused even the weakest from apathy, and called into play reserves of nervous force that we did not know we possessed. As for Captain Bligh, he displayed, throughout the whole of this night, a courage far above my poor powers to depict. Now and then his emaciated form would be clearly outlined for a second or two in a glare of lightning, then swallowed up in darkness. When I had said to Nelson, at Tofoa, that ours was a situation that Bligh was born to meet, I little realized how truthfully I spoke. Worn down though he was by hunger and hardship and lack of sleep, he showed no sign of weakening to the strain. Indeed, the more desperate our situation, the more he seemed to rejoice in it. I say this with no desire to exaggerate. He displayed on this night an exhilaration of mind the more striking in view of the peril of our situation. We passed through a series of violent squalls accompanied by thunder and lightning, and I shall never forget the vivid glimpses I had of him, one hand gripping the tiller, the other the gunwale, the seas that threatened to swamp us foaming up behind him and showering him with spray.

And I can still hear his voice in the darkness, heartening us all: "We're doing a full six knots, lads! Let that warm your blood if bailing can't do it—but don't stop bailing!"

Once, in a brief lull between storms, Fryer had suggested that a prayer be said. "No, Mr. Fryer," he replied. "Pray if you like, but to my way of thinking, God expects better than prayers of us at a time like this." It was in this same lull, I remember, that Cole called back, "Sir, shall I relieve you at the tiller?"

"Sit where you are, Mr. Cole," Bligh replied. "Do you think you can handle her better than myself?"

"I know very well I can't," Cole replied. "I was thinking how tired you must be."

A moment of silence followed; then we again heard Bligh's voice: "You are a good man, Mr. Cole, and an able man. I wish there were more like you in the service."

It was a handsome apology, and praise well deserved. I knew how it must have warmed Cole's heart.

The pause between squalls was of short duration. There was more, and worse, to come; and in the midst of it I saw Captain Bligh at the summit of his career.

There was a blinding glare of lightning, followed by a peal of thunder that seemed to shake the very bed of the deep. At that moment a great sea flung the launch into an all but vertical position. And there sat Bligh as on a throne, lifted high above us all, exalted in more than a physical sense.

"Bail, lads!" he shouted. "By God! We're beating the sea itself!"

CHAPTER VIII

DURING the following night the severity of the weather relaxed; at dawn the sea was so calm that for the first time in fifteen days we found it unnecessary to bail. I had managed to sleep for two or three hours in a miserably cramped position. When I awoke, I lay without moving for some time, gazing in a kind of stupor at what I could see of the others in the boat.

Nelson lay beside me. His eyes were half opened, and with his parted lips, looking blue in the morning light, his hollow cheeks and sunken temples, I thought for a moment, until aware of some slight sign of breathing, that he must have died during the night. Captain Bligh sat in the stern, beside Elphinstone, who held the tiller. Although reduced, like the rest of us, to skin and bone, and clad, like ourselves, in sodden rags, there was nothing grotesque in his appearance. Wear what he might, he was still a noble figure, and suffering but added to the dignity and firmness of his bearing.

"Come up here in the sun, Mr. Ledward," he said. "It will make a new man of you."

I struggled to stand, but was unable to rise. Mr. Bligh helped me to the seat beside him. He made a sign to Hayward and Tinkler to help Nelson up. The botanist gave me a ghastly smile, designed to be cheerful.

"I feel better already," he remarked in a weak voice.

The captain now addressed all hands. "Luck's with us," he said; "we've left the bad weather behind. Off with your cloathes, before the sun gets too high, and give them a drying while you've the chance. The sun on our bare hides will be as good as a glass of grog. . . . Mr. Samuel, issue a teaspoonful of rum all round!" He glanced about at the people appraisingly, and then added: "We'll celebrate the good weather, lads! An ounce of pork with our bread and water!"

Our cloathing, reduced to rags by soaking in rain and wringing out in sea water, was hung along the gunwales to dry, and we now presented a strange and pitiful spectacle. Our skins, from long soaking in the rain, looked dead white, like the bellies of fish; some of the men were so reduced that I thought it a wonder they were able to stand. Nothing was more remarkable than their cheerfulness in bearing their afflictions. The warm sun, not yet high enough to scorch us, was exceedingly grateful, and our breakfast, enriched by a bit of pork, was a cheerful meal.

The morning was as beautiful as any I have known

at sea. The breeze, at E.N.E., ruffled the sea to that shade of dark blue only to be seen between the tropics, and filled our sails bravely, without being boisterous enough to shower us with spray. The sky was clear save for the small, tufted, fair-weather clouds on the verge of the horizon.

Mr. Fryer reached over the side and brought up a bit of coconut husk, on which the first green beginnings of marine growth appeared. He handed it to the captain, who examined it with interest.

"This has been removed by man," he remarked. "And look! It has not been overlong in the sea! We're close in with New Holland, not a doubt of it!"

Nelson took it shakily from Bligh's hand. "Aye, the nut was husked by Indians on a pointed stake. The growth of weed sprouts quickly in these warm seas."

"Look!" exclaimed Elphinstone, pointing off to starboard.

Our heads turned, and we saw a company of the small black terns called noddies, flying this way and that, low over the sea as they searched for fish.

"Now, by God!" said the captain. "The land is not far off!"

The birds swung away to the west and disappeared. They were of the size of pigeons, and their flight resembled a pigeon's flight.

"The worst of our voyage is over," said Bligh.

"We shall be inside the reefs before the weather changes. You have borne yourselves like true English seamen so far; I am going to ask for further proofs of fortitude. I do not know certainly that there is a European settlement on Timor, and should there prove to be none, it would be imprudent to trust ourselves among the Indians there. For this reason, I think all hands will agree that we had best reduce our rations still further, in order to be able to reach Java if necessary. My task is to take you to England. To make sure of success, we must, from now on, do without our issue of bread for supper."

I glanced at the men covertly, knowing that some were so reduced that they might consider that Captain Bligh was cutting off the means of life itself. I was surprised and pleased, therefore, to see with what cheerfulness the captain's proposal was received.

"What's a twenty-fifth of an ounce of bread, sir?" asked old Purcell, grimly. "I 've no complaint! I 'd as soon have none as what we get. I reckon I could fetch Java with no bread at all!"

Bligh gave a short, harsh laugh. "By God, I believe you might!" he said.

"Once inside the reefs," remarked Nelson, "we 'll need little bread. There 'll be shellfish, and no doubt we shall find various fruits and berries on the islets."

Tinkler smacked his lips, and grinned. Like the other midshipmen, he had withstood the hardships better than the grown men. Even Hallet seemed to have grown but little thinner.

I had violent pains in my stomach throughout this day and suffered much from tenesmus, as did nearly every man in the boat. Two or three were constantly at the gunwales, attempting what they were never able to perform, for not one of us, since leaving the *Bounty*, had had evacuation by stool. At nightfall I lay down in the bilges in a kind of stupor, till dawn. I was awakened by Bligh's voice.

"Don't move!" he said.

Then I heard the voice of Smith, from the bows: "I'll have him next time."

I opened my eyes and saw a small, black bird pass overhead, looking down at the boat. Nelson was already awake, and whispered weakly: "A noddy! Twice he's made as if to alight on the stem!"

"Hush!" said the captain, looking down at us.

The little tern passed overhead once more, set his wings, and slanted down in the direction of the bow. Next moment I heard a feeble shout go up from the people, and the sound of fluttering wings.

"Good lad!" said Bligh to the man forward. "Don't wring his neck!"

I managed to pull myself up to a sitting position while they were passing a wineglass to Smith, who held the bird while Hall cut its throat, allowing the blood to flow into the small glass, which was filled nearly to the brim.

"Now pluck him," said Bligh, while the glass was being handed aft. He motioned the midshipmen to help Nelson to sit up. "For you, Mr. Nelson," he went on, giving Tinkler the glassful of blood.

Nelson smiled and shook his head. "Lamb and Simpson need it more than I. Give it to them."

"I order you to drink the blood," said Bligh, with a smile that robbed the words of sternness. . . . "Mr. Hayward, hold the glass for Mr. Nelson while he drinks."

The botanist closed his eyes and took the blood with a slight grimace, raising a trembling hand to wipe his lips. The youngsters made him as comfortable as they could by propping his back against the thwart.

Fryer was at the tiller. The plucked noddy, no larger than a small pigeon, was now handed to Mr. Bligh, who laid it on the carpenter's chest, took a knife from his pocket, and divided the bird into eighteen portions. It was done with the utmost possible fairness, though a sixth portion of the breast was preferable to one of the feet, and I should have preferred the neck to the head and beak.

"Come aft, Mr. Peckover," said the captain. . . . "Face forward, Mr. Cole, and call out when Mr. Peckover gives the word."

The boatswain turned so that he was unable to see what went on. Peckover looked over the shares of raw bird and took up a choice bit of the breast.

"Who shall have this?" he called.

"Mr. Bligh!" replied Cole.

"No! No!" the captain interrupted. "There must be no precedence here, Mr. Cole: you will begin with anyone's name, at random. Should we catch another bird, the order must be changed. The purpose of this old custom is to be fair to all."

Peckover laid down the bit of breast and took up a wing. "Who shall have this?"

"Peter Lenkletter!"

The wing was handed to the quartermaster. When Bligh's turn came, he was so unfortunate as to get a foot with nothing on it but the web, and a shred or two of sinew where it had been disjointed, but he gnawed this miserable portion with every appearance of relish, and threw away nothing but the barest bones. The head and beak fell to me; and it amazes me, as I write, to recollect with what enjoyment I swallowed the eyes, and crunched the little skull between my teeth as I sucked out the raw brains. Small as the amount of nourishment was, I fancied that it brought me an immediate increase of strength. I was happy when Nelson got a rich, red morsel of the breast. He wished to share it with me, and when I refused, he lingered long over it. "The noddy eats well!" he said. "No pheasant at home ever seemed better flavoured!"

Lamb was one of those men who seem born to make the worst of every misfortune; he was unable to sit

up, and had scarcely enough strength to complain of
the pain in his bowels. When his turn came, he
got the other foot; and Cole, who had just received
a portion of breast, handed it to him. "Here," he
said gruffly. "Ye need this more than me."

"Thankee, Mr. Cole, thankee!" said Lamb in a
quavering voice as he stuffed the bit of flesh into his
mouth.

The weather continued fair throughout the day,
with a calm sea and a good sailing breeze at E.N.E.
It was fortunate that we were not obliged to bail,
for many of us could not have undertaken the task.
Our log showed that we were making between four
and four and a half knots. During the afternoon
we passed bits of driftwood on which the barnacles
had not yet gathered, and Elphinstone picked up a
bamboo pole, such as the Indians use for fishing rods.
It was slimy with the beginnings of marine growth,
but could not have been more than two or three
weeks in the sea. Purcell took the bamboo, dried
and cleaned it, sawed off the ends square, and set to
fitting and seizing a worn-out file into the larger end,
to make a spear for fish.

Toward evening, a lone booby appeared astern, and
circled the boat for a long time, as if he desired to
alight. We sat in suspense for ten minutes or more.
The bird was not unlike our gannets at home, with a
body as great as that of a large duck, and a five-foot
spread of wings. I held my breath each time his

shadow passed over the boat; I could hear Bligh's hearty, whispered curses when the bird came sailing in as if to alight and then slanted away.

At last young Tinkler whispered: "Let me try, sir —with the bamboo. I've seen the Indians at Otaheite take them so, by breaking their wings."

Bligh nodded. The bird had again turned away. The youngster crept forward, took the spear from Purcell, and stood on a thwart. The booby swung back toward the boat, while Tinkler waved his bamboo back and forth gently. It was strange, as the bird turned back toward the launch, to see how the moving spear aroused his curiosity. He came on with a rapid flap of wings, turning his head to see better, and passed over us very low, though still too high to be reached. Tinkler continued to move the rod gently.

This time the booby did not rise, but turned and headed back. The youngster held the spear with both hands, ready to strike. On came the bird, lower than ever, his wings held rigidly. Tinkler raised the rod to the full extent of his arms, and struck. The blow caught the booby where one of the wings joined the body, and with a grating cry he plunged into the sea.

"Hard up!" shouted Captain Bligh.

For the first time since leaving Tofoa, the boat was turned into the wind. Her sails fluttered as she luffed and lost steerageway; we made a board and

came about on the other tack before we were able
to pick up the bird.

"By God, Mr. Tinkler," said the captain; "your
fishing with the Indians was not wasted time!"

The launch shot up into the wind. Many eager
hands went over the gunwale to pick up the wounded
bird. Lebogue caught him and tossed him into the
boat.

This time the blood was shared amongst Nelson,
Lamb, and Simpson, who received a full wineglass
each; and when the carcass — legs, head, bones, entrails, and flesh — was apportioned by the method
of "Who shall have this?" our shares were of a size
to make us feel that we were sitting down to a feast.
Three flying fish, each about seven inches long, were
found in the bird's stomach; they were fresh, and I
was overjoyed when one fell to me. I had eaten the
raw fish prepared by the Indians of Otaheite, and
found it palatable when dipped in a sauce of sea
water. I now opened my knife and scaled the flying fish gloatingly, before cutting it into morsels
which I dropped into the salt water in my coconut
shell. Nothing was wasted; I even ate the entrails,
and quaffed off the bloody salt water in which the fish
had soaked.

Though we sailed well, the weather remained serene
that day and during the two days following. On
Tuesday we passed fresh coconut husks and driftwood
which appeared to have been in the water no more

than a week.   We had the good fortune to catch three boobies on this day; without their blood and raw flesh I am convinced that two or three of us must have succumbed.   The sun was so hot at midday that I felt faint and sick.   On Wednesday it was apparent to all that the land was close ahead.   The clouds to the west were fixed, and there were innumerable birds about, though we could catch none.   The heat of the sun again caused much suffering.

"Soak what rags you can spare in the sea, and make turbans of them!" said the captain, when he heard some of the people complaining of the heat.   He laughed.   "English seamen are hard to please!   I'd rather be hot than cold any day, and dry than wet, for that matter!   Wring out your turbans frequently.   The cool water'll soon make you feel like fighting cocks.   We should sight the reefs to-morrow, with this breeze."

The boatswain smacked his lips.   "There'll be fine pickings, sir, once we find a passage.   Cockles, and clams, and who knows what!"

"We'll find a way in, never fear.   From our latitude, we should sight the land close to Providential Channel, through which Captain Cook sailed the *Endeavour.*"

Nelson lay on the floor boards, listening to the talk as coolly as if dining with the captain aboard the *Bounty.*

"From what I have heard Captain Cook say," he

remarked, "there must be many passages leading in to the sheltered water. No doubt we shall have several to choose from."

"So I believe," said Bligh.

At about nine o'clock that night, the captain lay down beside me to sleep.

"Keep a sharp lookout, Mr. Cole," he said; "we may be closer to the reefs than we suppose."

A swell from the east had set in, but the breeze was steady and light, and there were no whitecaps to wet us with spray. I lay half in a doze, half in a stupor, for several hours, listening to Bligh's quiet breathing. At last I fell asleep.

It must have been a little past midnight when I was awakened by the boatswain's voice: —

"Mr. Bligh! Breakers, sir!"

In an instant the captain was on his feet and wide awake. I heard a distant, long-drawn roar; and Bligh's abrupt command: "Hard alee!"

Three or four others were up by this time, ready for duty.

"Close-haul her!"

The moon was down, but the breakers were visible in the starlight as we clawed off.

"She lays well clear," remarked the captain. "By God! What a surf! Let it break! We'll find a way through when daylight comes!"

Many of us in the bottom of the boat were too

weak or too indifferent even to raise our heads. Bligh noticed that I stirred.

"The reefs of New Holland, Mr. Ledward! We'll be sailing calm water soon, and stretching our legs ashore! You'll be feasting on shellfish to-morrow, my word on it!"

I managed to turn on my side, and fell asleep once more, lulled by a new sound: the crisp slap of wavelets under the launch's bow as she stood off the land, close-hauled on the starboard tack.

At dawn, though the night had been warm and calm, most of the people were dreadfully weak. The birds we had eaten had merely prolonged our lives, without imparting any real strength. At the first signs of daylight, Mr. Bligh gave word to slack away to the west, but it was mid-morning before we again sighted the breakers. The wind had shifted to S.E. during the night.

Two teaspoons of rum were issued before we drank our water and ate our scant mouthful of bread. Heartened by the spirit and the prospect of smooth water and food, I struggled to a sitting position. Nelson was unable to sit up. Mr. Bligh had poured a few drops of rum between his lips, but he had shaken his head weakly when offered bread. I could see that the botanist, for all his courage, was at the end of his tether; unless we could secure fresh food for him, another day or two would see him dead.

Lamb and Simpson were in a piteous state, and several others were nearly as bad.

Toward nine o'clock a line of tossing white stretched away as far as we could see to the north and south. The vast roll of the Pacific, broken by the coral barrier, thundered and spouted furiously.

Not more than a hundred yards beyond the first break of the seas, Bligh steered to the north, ordering Tinkler and Cole to trim the sheets.

"There, lads!" he said. "That should put heart in you! Never fear! We shall soon be inside!"

It was indeed a strange and heartening sight to men in our situation to see, just beyond the barrier of furious breakers, the placid waters of a vast lagoon, scarce ruffled by the gentle southeast breeze. And it seemed to me that I could perceive the outlines of land, blue and misty in the distance, far away across the calm water.

We had rounded a point of the reef and coasted for some distance in a northwesterly direction, when it fell calm for a few moments and the wind chopped around to east. Bligh bore up and ordered the sails trimmed once more, when we perceived that the reefs jutted far out to sea ahead of us.

"Forward with you, Mr. Cole!" said Bligh, and, when the boatswain stood in the bows with a hand on the foremast, "Can she lay clear?"

Cole gazed ahead intently for a moment before he replied: "No, sir! Can't ye point up a bit?"

Though close-hauled, the luff of the mainsail was shivering a little at the time. Bligh shrugged his shoulders. "Hard alee!" he ordered. "Let go the halyards and get her on the other tack!"

We had not sailed a quarter of a mile on the larboard tack, when it was evident that we were embayed. The east wind had caught us unaware, and we could not lay clear of the points to north or south. We turned the launch north once more.

"Who can pull an oar?" Bligh asked.

Lenkletter, Lebogue, and Elphinstone attempted to rise, and sank back ashamed of their weakness. Fryer, Purcell, Cole, and Peckover took their places at the thwarts. They pulled grimly and feebly; in spite of their courage, they had not sufficient strength to enable us to clear the point of reef about two miles ahead.

"Now, by God!" Bligh exclaimed. "We must weather the point or shoot the breakers — one of the two! . . . Mr. Tinkler! Are you strong enough to steer? Take the tiller and point up as close as you can!"

The captain set a tholepin on the lee side, ran out an oar, and began to pull strongly and steadily.

The prospect of shooting the breakers was enough to make the hardiest seaman pause. I could see, from time to time, the dark, jagged coral of the reef, revealed by a retreating sea. A moment later the same spot would be buried deep in foaming water, rushing over the reef with the thunder of a mighty cataract. It was incredible that our boat, small and deep laden, could live for an instant in such a turmoil. As I glanced ahead my heart sank. Then Tinkler shouted: —

"Mr. Bligh! There's a passage ahead, sir! Well this side of the point!"

Bligh shipped his oar and rose instantly. After a quick glance ahead, he turned to the men. "Cease pulling, lads," he said kindly. "Providence has been good to us. Yonder lies our channel; we can fetch it under sail."

CHAPTER IX

THE passage was less than a mile ahead, and as we were now able to bear off a little and fill the sails, we were abreast of the opening in about a quarter of an hour. It proved to be a good two cable-lengths wide, and clear of rocks, with a small, barren islet just inside. We entered with a strong current setting to the westward; presently the roll of the sea was gone, and the launch sailed briskly over waters as calm as those of a lake at home.

I looked with longing at the islet close abreast of us. Though small and barren, it was at least dry land. Purcell's longing got the better of him.

"Let us go ashore, sir," he suggested, when it was apparent that the captain was going to sail on. "Cannot we land and stretch our legs?"

Bligh shook his head. "We should find nothing there. Look ahead, man!"

Two other islands, one of them high and wooded, were now visible at a distance of four or five leagues to the northwest; and close beyond, I could see the main of New Holland — valleys and high land, densely wooded in parts.

The afternoon was well advanced when we reached

the first of the two islands—little more than a heap
of stones. The larger island was about three miles in
circuit, high, well wooded, with a sheltered, sandy
bay on the northwest side. From this bay, the nearest
point on the main was about four hundred yards distant. As there were no signs of Indians in the vicinity, we beached the boat at once. For twenty-six
days we had not set foot on land.

Mr. Bligh was the first to step on shore, staggering
a little from weakness and the unaccustomed feel of
firm ground. Fryer, Purcell, Peckover, Cole, and
the midshipmen followed. All these could walk,
though with difficulty. Hall, Smith, Lebogue and
Samuel managed to get out of the boat, and either
staggered or crawled to a place where the sand was
soft and shaded by some small, bushy trees. The rest
of us were in such a state as forced our stronger
companions to help us ashore.

Mr. Bligh now uncovered, while those who were
able knelt round him on the sand; and if ever men
have offered heartfelt thanks to God for deliverance
from the perils of the sea, surely we were those men.

After a brief silence, Bligh cleared his throat and
turned to the master. "Mr. Fryer," he said, "take
the strongest of the people and search for shellfish.
There should be oysters or mussels on the rocks
yonder. . . . Mr. Peckover, you will accompany
me inland. . . . Mr. Cole, remain in charge of the
boat. Take care that no fires are lit to-night."

Nelson and I had each had a small sup of wine, administered by the captain's hand. This, together with the prospect of something to eat and the delight of being once more on land, gave us fresh strength. We lay side by side. The sand was pleasantly warm, and a clump of dwarfish palms cast an agreeable shade.

We talked but little. We needed time to accustom ourselves to the fact that we were still alive, and to lie outstretched on dry land was a privilege so great that we could scarcely believe it ours.

"Can you realize, my dear Ledward, that our troubles are over?" Nelson asked, at length. "I have often heard Captain Cook speak of his passage inside the reefs of New Holland. Among these islands we shall find something to eat: shellfish, certainly, as well as berries and beans that are fit for food. There should be water on some of the larger islands."

"It is curious," I replied; "at present I feel not the slightest desire for food. I would not exchange the rest we are enjoying for the best meal that might be set before us."

"I feel the same," he said. "It is rest we need now above everything."

We fell silent again, and remained so for a long time. A flock of large birds, parrots of some sort, passed overhead with harsh cries and disappeared in the direction of the main. I saw Nelson's eyes roving this way and that as he studied the vegetation about us.

"These palms are new to me," he said; "yet I feel certain that their hearts, like those of the coconut palm, will provide excellent salad."

Presently the sun went down, and far along the beach we saw the foraging party returning. I knew how weary they must be, and felt ashamed of my own lack of strength.

"We're a useless pair, Nelson," I said. "Why were we not given stronger bodies?"

"Never fear," he replied. "We'll soon be taking our share of labour. I feel greatly refreshed already."

The captain and Peckover had their hats partly filled with fruits of two sorts.

"Have a look at these, Mr. Nelson," said Bligh. "By God! We've found little for the length of the walk. I observed that the birds eat freely of these berries. May we not do the same?"

"Aye, they look wholesome and good. I recognize their families, but the species are new to me. These palms, sir — cannot some of the people cut out a few of the hearts? We'll find them delicious, I'll be bound."

"There, Peckover!" Bligh exclaimed, turning to the gunner. "That shows the need for a botanist in every ship's company. We've walked miles for a few berries, and Mr. Nelson finds food for us within a dozen paces of the boat!"

"Aye," said Peckover. "I'd be pleased to have the knowledge inside Mr. Nelson's head. We've found good water, Mr. Ledward, and plenty of it. We can drink our fill while here."

Fryer and his men were coming up the beach — well laden, as I perceived at a glance.

"We shall feast to-night," he called. "We've found oysters galore! And larger and better tasting than those at home!"

"Come, lads," said Bligh; "let us turn to without waste of time."

I have never been averse to the pleasures of the table, and have had the good fortune to partake of many excellent meals; but never do I recollect having supped with more pleasure than on this night. Fryer had adopted the simple expedient of opening the oysters where they grew, without attempting to loose them from the rocks. Our copper pot held close to three gallons, and it was more than half full of oysters of an amazing size, soaking in their own juice. Some of the people had woven baskets of palm fronds, an art they had learned from the Indians of Otaheite, and in these they carried a supply of unopened oysters, prized off the rocks with a cutlass. The fruits were excellent, particularly one kind which resembled a gooseberry, but tasted sweeter; the palm hearts were like tender young cabbage, eaten raw.

I recommended Nelson, Lamb, and Simpson to eat

of nothing but oysters that night,—a diet suitable
to their distressed state,—and I myself refrained
from anything else.   The night was warm and clear.
When we had supped, and drunk to our heart's content of the cool, sweet water of the island, I composed
myself for sleep on the sand.

The firm ground seemed still to rock and heave.
But it was wonderfully agreeable to stretch my legs
out to their full extent; to lie on the warm sand and
gaze up at the stars.   I was sorry for some of the people, who had been ordered to anchor the launch in
shallow water, near the sands, and to sleep aboard
of her.   Mr. Bligh thought it not unlikely that Indians might be about.   Presently I closed my eyes to
thank my Maker briefly for His goodness in preserving us; a few moments later I fell into a dreamless
sleep.

I was awakened by the loud chattering of parrots,
flying from the interior of our island, where they appeared to roost, to the main.   Flock after flock passed
overhead with a great clamour; the last of them had
gone before the sun was up.   My companions lay
sleeping close by, in the attitudes they had assumed
the night before.   I saw the boatswain wade ashore
from the launch and kneel on the wet sand while he
repeated the Lord's Prayer in a rumbling voice,
plainly audible where I lay.   He rose, stripped off his
shirt and ragged trousers, and plunged into the shallow bay, scrubbing his head and shoulders vigor-

ously. Longing to follow his example, I managed to struggle to my feet, and was pleased to discover that I could walk.

Still splashing in the sea, Cole greeted me. "No need to ask how ye slept, Mr. Ledward! Ye look a new man!"

I felt one when I had bathed in the cool sea water and resumed my tattered garments, which a London ragpicker would have scorned to accept. The others were rising as I turned inland, walking with the uncertain gait of a year-old child.

Nelson managed to stand at the second attempt, but was forced to sink down again immediately, doubled up with a sharp pain in his stomach. "By God!" he said with a wry smile. "I've a mind to ask you to physic me."

I shook my head. "It would be imprudent in our state of weakness. Our pain and tenesmus are due to the emptiness of our bowels."

Bligh joined us at that moment. "Sound advice, sir," he said; "if a layman may express an opinion. To physic men in our state would but weaken us still more. I have suffered from the same violent pains. We'll be quit of them once our bellies are filled." He turned to hail the boatswain. "Come ashore, Mr. Cole, the lot of you."

Fryer was sent out with a party to get oysters, and two men dispatched inland for fruit. Cole and Purcell were set to putting the boat in order, in case we should find savages about. I was among four or five whom the captain ordered to rest throughout the morning. Nelson lay beside me in the shade.

"What the devil is Cole up to?" he remarked.

The boatswain was wading about the launch, moving in circles and staring down into the water. After some time he came ashore with a long face. Bligh was writing in his journal, and glanced up as Cole addressed him.

"The lower gudgeon of the rudder's gone, sir," he said. "It must have dropped off as we was entering the bay. It's not on the sand — that I'll vouch for."

Bligh closed his journal with a snap, and stood up. "Unship the rudder. Are you sure it's nowhere under the boat?"

"I've made certain of that, sir."

"Then lend Mr. Purcell a hand." He turned to Nelson. "We've Providence to thank that this did not happen a few days ago! I had grummets fixed on either side of the transom, as you observed, in case we were forced to steer with the oars; but in severe weather it would have been next to impossible to keep afloat with them. We should have broached-to, almost certainly."

Presently the carpenter brought the rudder ashore.

"It's been under heavy strains, sir," he explained. "The screws holding the gudgeon to the sternpost must have loosened in the wood."

"Well, what can be done?"

Purcell held out a large staple. "I found this under the floor boards. It will serve."

"Do your best, and see that it is stoutly set. We must beach the boat and examine her bottom to-day."

The captain took leave of us and wandered inland to search for fruit. Purcell hammered at his staple on a rock, fitting its curve to the pintle of the rudder. I recommended the invalids to drink frequently of water, taking as much as they could hold, and set them an example by doing the same.

"It's grub I need, not water!" said Lamb, making a wry face as I handed him a coconut-shell full.

"You'll have plenty of that shortly, my lad!" I said.

Simpson crawled off for another useless attempt to perform the impossible. "Poor devil!" Nelson said. "I'll soon be doing the same."

A little before noon the oyster gatherers returned with a bountiful supply. Nelson and I had arranged a hearth of stones, and found strength to gather a quantity of firewood. Bligh was soon on hand to kindle the fire with his magnifying glass and supervise the making of the stew — our first taste of hot food since leaving Tofoa, nearly a month before. The people were gathered in a circle about our fireplace, staring at the pot like a pack of wolves.

When all the oysters had been opened, we found that they and their liquor filled the pot to within four inches of the brim. Captain Bligh ordered Samuel

to weigh out a twenty-fifth of a pound of bread
for each man, making three quarters of a pound in
all. A pound of fat pork was now cut up very
fine and thrown into the stew, already beginning to
bubble over a brisk fire. I was sitting with Nelson
on the lee side, inhaling savoury whiffs of steam that
drifted past.

"Let us add a quart of sea water," said the master
to Mr. Bligh. "It will serve as salt, and make the
stew go further."

"No, Mr. Fryer. What with oysters and the pork,
it will be salty enough as it is."

"We could add fresh water to make more of it.
There 'll not be enough to go round."

"Not enough, with a full pint each?" said Bligh
impatiently. "If it will do for me, it will do for
yourself, sir."

Fryer said no more.

Presently the stew was ready. It was served out
in Bligh's own coconut shell, known to hold exactly
a pint. My own shell held double that, and when
I had been served I wished with the master that the
amount might have been more. The crumbled bits
of bread had boiled down to mingle with the liquor
from the oysters and the fat pork, forming a sauce
an alderman might not have despised. I tasted a
small quantity with a little spoon I had whittled out of
a bit of driftwood.

"Damme, sir!" said Bligh, turning to Nelson.

"Many's the time I've eaten worse than this on His Majesty's ships."

"And many a better meal you have enjoyed less, I dare say," Nelson replied.

"I've served on ships," said Fryer, "where we'd not such a meal for six months together."

"Aye," said the captain. "Hunger's the only sauce. It was damn near worth starving for a month to have such a relish for victuals. . . . Do you mind what day it is, Mr. Nelson?"

"What day? I could not be sure of telling you within a week."

"It is Friday, the twenty-ninth of May: the anniversary of the Restoration of King Charles the Second. We shall call this Restoration Island, in his memory. The name will serve in a double sense. *We* have been restored, God knows!"

Employing some self-restraint, I managed to eat my share so as to take a full half hour to finish it. Fryer, I observed, gulped his down in an instant, and held out his shell for the few spoonfuls left over for every man. Purcell and Lenkletter played the gluttons as well, and I was forced to warn Simpson, still in a very weak state, against swallowing his food too fast.

Nelson and I felt so much revived after dinner that we set out for a tottering walk into the island. We found it rocky, with a barren soil, supporting a growth of stunted trees. There were many of the small palms whose hearts we had found good to eat; I recognized the *purau*, of Otaheite, in a stunted form; and there were other trees which Nelson informed me resembled the poisonous manchineel of the West Indies. About the summit of the island, not above one hundred and fifty feet in height, great numbers of parrots and large pigeons were feeding on the berries here growing in abundance, but though we tried to knock them down with stones, the birds were as hard to approach as partridges in England. We gathered a quantity of the better sort of berries, which eat very well indeed, and as we wandered toward the eastern side of the island we came upon two tumbled-down huts of the Indians. These were ruder than any Indian habitations I had seen. Nelson stooped over the blackened stones of a fireplace to take up a roughly fashioned spear, with the sharp end hardened in the fire.

At that moment I perceived in the sand the tracks of some large animal, unlike the footprints of any beast known to me. Nelson examined the tracks with interest.

"I think I can name the beast," he said; "Mr. Gore, Captain Cook's lieutenant, shot one at Endeavour River, south of here. It was as great as a man, mouse-coloured, and ran hopping on its hind legs. The Indians called it *kanguroo*."

"How could it have come here?" I asked. "Do they swim?"

"That I don't know. Perhaps; or it may be that the Indians stock these islands with young ones, where they may be easily caught when required."

"Is the flesh fit for food?"

"Cook thought it was good as the best mutton. The beasts are said to be timid, and to run faster than a horse."

As we approached the rocky shore on the east side of the island, Nelson chose himself a long, wide palm frond, and sat down, Indian fashion, to plait a basket. I admired the deftness of his fingers as they wove the leaflets swiftly this way and that; in ten minutes he had completed a stout basket, handle and all, fit to hold a full bushel.

"Now for the shellfish!" he remarked, as he rose shakily to his feet. "Gad, Ledward! I feel a new man to-day!"

I set to work with the cutlass, opening the oysters growing here and there on the rocks below high-water mark; with his Indian spear, Nelson waded among the pools. I soon had three or four dozen oysters in the basket. Nelson added two large cockles of the Tridacna kind to our bag: the pair of them a meal for a man. It was mid-afternoon when we took up our burdens and trudged back to the encampment, halting frequently to rest.

Our stew that afternoon was a noble one—oysters, cockles, and chopped-up heart of palm. This latter was added at Nelson's suggestion, and was the cause of some murmuring.

"Are we to have no bread, sir?" asked the carpenter sourly.

"No," replied Captain Bligh; "we shall save our bread. Mr. Nelson says these palm hearts are as good cooked as raw."

Fryer stood by with a gloomy face. "It will ruin the stew," he said. "The bread was the making of it at dinner time."

"Aye, sir," put in Purcell, "give us but half the full amount. It'll be poor stuff without the bread."

Bligh turned away impatiently. "Damn it, *no!*" he replied. "You're grown queasy as young ladies on the island here! Wait till you taste the stew, if you must complain."

Our meal was soon pronounced done, and each man received a full pint and a half. The sauce seemed to me even better than that we had eaten at dinner, and once the men tasted it all murmuring ceased.

At sunset, when it fell dead calm, we observed several columns of smoke at a distance of two or three miles on the main. Bligh ordered some of the people to pass the night in the boat, and a watch was kept on shore.

"We must be on our guard," he said; "though I believe there is small danger of the Indians visiting us to-night. Our fire made no smoke, and they cannot have seen the boat."

As darkness came on, Bligh went down to the beach, where Cole was on watch, and remained for a long time seated on the sand chatting with him, while the rest of us retired to our sleeping places.

Nelson was asleep almost at once; but returning strength had left me wakeful, and I lay for a long time gazing at the starlit sky. Purcell and the master lay close by, conversing in low tones. Perhaps they thought me asleep; in any event, I could not avoid overhearing what they said. After a time, I perceived that their talk had turned to the mutiny.

"Ungrateful?" the carpenter was saying. "Damn my eyes! What had they to be grateful for? Christian was treated worse than a dog half the time. I excuse none of 'em, mind! I'd be pleased to see every man of the lot swinging at a yardarm; but I'll say this: If ever a captain deserved to lose his ship, ours did."

"If that's your feeling, why didn't you join with Christian?" said Fryer.

"It's no love for Captain Bligh that kept me from it, I'll promise you that," said Purcell. "He's himself to thank for the mutiny, and so I'll say if we've the luck to get home."

"He has his faults," said Fryer. "He trusts none of his officers to perform their duties, but must have a hand in everything. But if you think him a Tartar, you should sail with some of the captains I've served under. There was old Sandy Evans! The last topman off the main yard got half a dozen with a colt. He called it 'encouraging' them."

"I'd rather be flogged than cursed before my own men," growled Purcell. "You mind what he called me before my mates in Adventure Bay? And what he said to Christian, with all the people about, the day before they seized the ship?"

"He's overfree with his tongue," admitted Fryer. "But what captain is not? The Navy's no place for thin skins. Hard words and floggings are what seamen understand." He paused for a moment. "I've served under easier captains," he added. "He's a hard man to please. But where would we be without him now? Tell me that. Whom would you wish in his place in the launch?"

"I'm not saying he lacks his good points," the carpenter admitted grudgingly.

When I fell asleep at last, their voices were still murmuring on. I awoke feeling better than for many days past. Nelson was already up, and a party was setting out down the beach in search of new beds of oysters. Bligh was speaking to Purcell.

"I saw some good *purau* trees near the summit of the island," he said. "Take your axe and see if you can find us a pair of spare gaffs."

He turned to the boatswain. "Mr. Cole, see that the casks are all filled and placed in the boat."

I went off oystering with Nelson, both of us able to walk pretty well by now. When we returned,

preparations for dinner were under way. Mr. Bligh
held in his hand the last of our pork, a piece of about
two pounds' weight, well streaked with lean. He
handed it to Hall, motioning him to cut it up for the
pot.

"We'll sail with full bellies," he remarked. "Since
some villain robbed his mates of their pork, we'll put
it out of his power to play that scurvy trick again."

He looked hard at Lamb as he spoke, and it seemed
to me that the man hung his head with some slight expression of guilt.

With plenty of oysters, about a couple of ounces of
pork for each man, and the usual ration of bread,
we dined sumptuously; had we had a little pepper to
season it, the stew would have been pronounced excellent anywhere. We had scarce finished eating
when the captain spoke: —

"We shall set sail about two hours before sunset.
With this moon coming on, we can avoid the danger
of canoes by traveling as much as possible by night.
Mr. Nelson and I will remain to guard the launch;
the rest of you gather oysters for a sea store."

The master had just stretched out for a siesta after
his dinner, and he sat up with a gloomy expression
at Bligh's words.

"Can we not rest this afternoon, sir?" he asked.
"None of us has his full strength as yet, and surely
we shall find oysters at every landing place."

"Aye," growled Purcell. "You promised us we

should touch at many islands before clearing Endeavour Straits."

"I did," said the captain; "but what assurance have
you that we shall find oysters on them? We *know*
that there are plenty here." He flushed, controlling
his temper with some difficulty. "We've naught but
bread now, and little enough of that. Fetch what
oysters you wish, or none at all! I'm tired of your
damned complaints!" He turned his back and
walked away as if fearing to lose control of himself.
Shamed into acquiescence, Fryer and the carpenter
now joined the others setting out along the shore.

The captain's clerk was strolling southward with
a basket on his arm, and I joined him, since Nelson
was to remain with the boat.

"You know your Bible, Mr. Ledward," remarked
Samuel, when we were out of earshot of the others.
"Do you recollect the passage concerning Jeshurun
who waxed fat, and kicked?"

"Aye; and it falls pat on Restoration Island!"

Samuel smiled. "Where would they be, where
would we all be, without Captain Bligh? Yet they
must murmur the moment their bellies are full! I've
no patience with such men."

"Nor I." Glancing at the clerk's formerly plump
body, now reduced to little more than skin and bones,
and clad in rags, I could not repress a smile.

"Though we kick," I said, "none of us could be
accused of waxing fat!"

Toward four o'clock we returned with what shell-fish we had been able to secure, and found all in readiness to sail. We took our places in the launch, the grapnel was weighed, and we were getting sail on her, when about a score of Indians appeared on the opposite shore of the main, shouting loudly at us. The heads of many others were discernible above the ridge behind them; but, to our great content, they seemed to be unprovided with canoes. Owing to this fortunate circumstance, we were able to pass pretty close to them, with a fresh breeze at E.S.E. They carried long, slender lances in their right hands, and in their left hands some sort of weapon or implement of an oval shape and about two feet long.

These Indians were unlike any we had seen in the South Sea; they were coal black, tall, and remarkably thin, with long, skinny legs. Two of the men stood leaning on their spears, with one knee bent, and the sole of the foot pressed against the inside of the other thigh—an attitude comical as it was uncouth. Though too far off to distinguish their features clearly, they seemed to me quite as ugly as the natives of Van Diemen's Land.

The breeze freshened as we drew out of the lee, and the launch footed it briskly to the north, while the hallooing of savages grew fainter and finally died away.

CHAPTER X

RESTORATION ISLAND had proved well worthy of its name. It might as truthfully have been called Preservation Island, for there is no doubt whatever that, had we been delayed a day or two longer in reaching it, several of our number must have succumbed. Nelson and I would have been two of these; we were drawing upon our last reserves of strength when we passed through the channel into the great lagoons of New Holland. But, after three days of rest and a sufficiency of food, we were wonderfully restored; so much so, that we could take interest and pleasure in the scenes before us.

Ours was, in fact, a great privilege, and I was grateful for the fact that I had recovered strength enough to recognize it. We were coasting the shores of a mighty continent, through waters and among islands all but unknown to white men. Indeed, in so far as I knew, Captain Cook alone had passed this way before us. On our left lay the main, stretching away, we knew not how many hundreds or thousands of leagues, and wrapped in a silence that seemed to have lain there since the beginning of time — a deep, all-pervading stillness like that of mid-ocean on a calm day. Not one of us, I think, but felt the vastness of this presence.

We had in view a low, barren-looking coast that appeared a complete solitude, uninhabited and uninhabitable; and yet we knew, from our experience of the day before, that a few bands of savages, at least, must find sustenance there. We saw more of them before we had sailed many miles.

A number of small islands were in sight to the northeast. Captain Bligh directed our course between them and the main. The strait was no more than a mile wide, and as we were passing through it, a small party of savages like those we had already seen came down to the foreshore on our left hand and stood regarding us.

"Now," said Bligh, "I mean to have a closer view of those fellows."

Accordingly, we steered inshore and laid the boat as close as was prudent to the rocks. Meanwhile, the savages, observing our intent, had run away to a distance of about two hundred yards.

Bligh shouted: "Come aboard, there!" and stood in the stern sheets waving a shirt aloft; but not a foot would they stir from their places. They were without a vestige of cloathing, and their bodies looked as black as ink in the clear morning light, against a background of sand and naked rocks. Their timidity was encouraging in our unarmed and weakened condition; we felt that we had little to fear from any small bands of these people.

"They 'll never come," said Nelson, after we had lain at our oars shouting and beckoning to them. "It's a pity, too, for they seem harmless enough, and they must have ways of getting food that would be most valuable to us could we learn what they are."

"No, we may as well proceed," said Bligh. "I should like to see them near at hand. Sir Joseph Banks is most anxious to have a description of the savages of New Holland. He shall have to be content with the little I can tell him of their general appearance."

"That is a curious-looking instrument they carry in their left hands," I observed. "What can its purpose be?"

"In my opinion, it is some sort of a spear thrower," said Nelson. "One thing you can tell Sir Joseph," he added: "There are probably no savages in all the South Sea more ugly and uncouth than these. What a contrast they make to the Indians of Otaheite!"

We again hoisted sail, and steered for an island in view before us and about four miles distant from the main. This we reached in about an hour's time. The shore was rocky, but the water smooth. We made a landing without difficulty, and secured our boat in a little basin, where it rode in complete safety. We brought everything ashore, that the boat might be thoroughly cleaned and dried—putting our water vessels and the carpenter's chest, with its precious supply of bread, in the shelter of some overhanging rocks.

When we had scrubbed out the boat, Mr. Bligh told off two parties to go in search of shellfish. Purcell was placed in charge of one of these; the other members were Tinkler, Samuel, Smith, and Hall. These men stood waiting for the carpenter, who had seated himself on the beach with the air of one who meant to pass the day there. The other party, in Peckover's charge, had already gone southward along the beach. Captain Bligh, who had accompanied them a little distance, now returned to where the boat lay.

"Come, Mr. Purcell," he said brusquely; "set out at once with your men. We have no time to lose here."

The carpenter remained seated. "I've done more than my share of work," he said, in a surly voice. "You can send someone else with this party."

Bligh glared down at him. "Do you hear me?" he said. "Get you gone, and quickly!"

The carpenter made no motion to obey. "I'm as good a man as yourself," he replied; "and I'll stay where I am."

Nelson, the master, and myself, besides the members of the foraging party, were the witnesses of this scene. I had long expected something of the sort to happen, and had only wondered that an open break between Captain Bligh and the carpenter had not come before this time. There was a deep and natural antagonism between the two men; they were too much alike in character ever to have been anything but enemies.

Bligh strode across the beach to where the carpenter's chest had been placed, with two of the cutlasses lying upon it. Seizing the weapons, he returned to where Purcell sat and thrust one of them into his hand.

"Now," he said. "Stand up and defend yourself. Stand up, I say! If you are as good a man as myself, you shall prove it, here and now!"

There was no doubt of the seriousness of Bligh's intent. Despite the gravity of the situation, as I think of it now, there was something faintly comic in it as well. In the mind's eye I have the scene clearly in mind: The sandy spit of beach, backed by the naked rocks; the little group of spectators, their cloathes hanging in rags on their emaciated bodies, looking on at these two, who, despite starvation and hardships incredible, still had fight in them. At least, so I thought at first; but the carpenter quickly showed that his relish for it was faint indeed. He rose, holding his cutlass slackly, and gazed at Bligh with a frightened expression.

"Stand back, you others!" said Bligh. "Up with your weapon, you mutinous villain! I'll soon prove whether you are a man or not!"

He advanced resolutely toward the carpenter, who backed away at his approach.

"Fight, damn you!" Bligh roared. "Defend your-self or I'll cut you down as you stand!"

Purcell, although a larger man than Bligh, had little of the latter's inner fire and strength. Bligh was thoroughly roused; and had the carpenter tried to make good his boast, one or the other of them would, I am convinced, have been killed — and I have little doubt as to which would have been the victim. But Purcell made a complete about-face, and ran from his pursuer, who halted and gazed after him, breathing rapidly.

"Come back, Mr. Purcell!" he cried. "You have even less spirit than I gave you credit for! Come here, sir! . . . Now then; do you retract what you have said?"

"Yes, sir," Purcell replied.

"Very well," said Bligh. "Let me have no more of your insolence in the future. Get about your work."

It is to Bligh's credit that he never afterwards mentioned this incident. As for the carpenter, he was willing enough to have it forever put out of mind. He had, I believe, flattered himself that he was a match for his commander. From this time on, the relations of the two men were on a better footing.

The island upon which we had landed was of a considerable height. While the foraging parties were out, Mr. Bligh, Nelson, and myself walked inland to the highest part of it for a better view of our surroundings; but we could see little more of the main than appeared from below. In our weakened condition the climb had been a fatiguing one, and we took shelter in the shade of a great rock to recover our breath. The lagoons were miracles of vivid colouring in the clear morning light. We could plainly see the tiny figures of the foraging parties as they made their way slowly along the shallows, searching for shellfish. Almost directly below us was the launch, looking smaller than a child's toy in the bight where she lay.

"There she lies," said Bligh, gazing fondly at the tiny craft. "I love every strake of planking, every nail in her. Mr. Nelson, could you have believed that she could have carried eighteen men such a voyage as we have come? Could you, Mr. Ledward?"

"I was thinking of just that," Nelson replied. "We have been under God's guidance. It must have been so."

"Aye," said Bligh, nodding gravely. "But God expected us to play our part. We should not have had his help, otherwise."

"What distance have we come, in all, sir?" I asked.

"I have this morning reckoned it up," said Bligh. "I think I am not far out in saying that we have sailed, from Tofoa to the passage within the reefs of New Holland, a distance of two thousand, three hundred and ninety miles."

"God be thanked that we have so much of the

voyage behind us," said Nelson, fervently. "This
leaves us with one thousand miles ahead, does it not?"

"More than that," Bligh replied. "As nearly as I
can recollect, we have between one hundred and fifty
and two hundred miles to coast New Holland before
we reach Endeavour Straits; but once again in the
open sea, we shall have no more than three hundred
leagues between us and Timor."

Nelson turned to me. "Ledward, how long can a
man go, in the ordinary course of nature, without
passing stool?"

"Ten days is a long period under more normal circumstances," I replied, "but our situation is anything
but a usual one. We have had so little food that our
bodies seem to have absorbed the whole of it."

"So I think," said Bligh. "There could have been
nothing in our bowels until within a day or two
past. You look another man, Mr. Nelson, now that
you have had rest and better food. We shall all
have time to gain new strength before we push off
for Timor."

"I mean to survive," Nelson replied, smiling faintly;
"if only to defeat the purpose of the wretches who
condemned us to this misery."

"Spoken like a man, sir," said Bligh. A cold glint
came into his eyes and his lips were set in a thin line.
"By God! I could sail the launch to England, if
necessary, with nothing but water in my belly, for the
sake of bringing them to justice!"

He rose to his feet and strode back and forth across

the little flat-topped eminence where we rested; then he halted before us. Pale, hollow-eyed, his shreds of clothing hanging loosely upon his bones, he yet had within him a fund of energy that amazed me. Mention of the mutineers had stirred him as the call of a trumpet stirs an old cavalry horse. He laughed in his harsh mirthless way. "They flatter themselves that they have seen the last of me," he said; "the God-damned inhuman, black-hearted bastards! But Divine Providence sees them and will help me to track them down!"

Nelson threw a quick, quizzical glance in my direction. Bligh was quite unconscious of the mixture of blasphemy and reverence in his remark.

"Shall you endeavour to search for them yourself?" Nelson asked.

"Endeavour? By God, I shall more than endeavour! I shall sit on the doorstep at the Admiralty day and night until they give me command of the ship that is to search them out and bring them to justice. I have friends at home who will make my interest their own. I shall not draw a quiet breath until I am outward bound, on their trail."

"Your family may take a different view of the matter, sir," I said. "If we are fortunate enough to reach England, Mrs. Bligh will not wish to let you go so soon again."

"You know me little, Mr. Ledward, if you think I shall dawdle at home with those villains unhung.

Not a day shall I spend there if I have my way. As for Mrs. Bligh, she is no ordinary women. She will be the first to bid me God speed. . . . Let us go down," he added, after a moment of silence. "I grudge every moment that we are not proceeding on our way."

Nelson and I rose to follow him. Bligh stood looking toward a small sandy cay that could be seen at a considerable distance to the northward, and several miles farther from the main than the island upon which we then were.

"We shall go there for the night," he said. "It will be a safer resting place. The savages yonder must have seen us land here. They seem harmless enough; and yet, without weapons to defend ourselves, I mean to take no risks."

We went down by another way, to the northern side of the island, stopping now and then to examine the shrubs and stunted trees that grew out of the sand and among clefts in the rocks. We found nothing in the way of food except wild beans, which we gathered in a handkerchief.

"You are sure these are edible, Mr. Nelson?" Bligh asked.

"Yes, there is not the slightest danger," Nelson replied. "They are dolichos. The flavour is not all that might be wished, but the bean is a nourishing food. It is of the genus of the kidney bean to which the Indian gram belongs.'"

"Good," said Bligh. "Let us hope that the others have collected some as well as ourselves."

Upon reaching the beach, we discovered an old canoe lying bottom up and half buried in the sand. We dug away around it, but our combined strength was not sufficient to budge it, to say nothing of turning it over. It was about thirty feet long, with a sharp, projecting bow, rudely carved in the resemblance of a fish's head. We estimated that it would hold about twenty men.

"Here is proof enough," said Bligh, "that the New Hollanders are not wholly landlubbers. In view of this find, I am all the more willing to proceed farther from the main. We must keep a sharp lookout for these fellows. In our weakened condition they would find us an easy prey."

We were now joined by Purcell and his party of foragers, carrying our copper pot on a pole between them. They had had splendid luck—the pot was more than half full of fine, fat clams and oysters. Bligh put the carpenter at ease by greeting him in his usual manner.

"It couldn't be better, Mr. Purcell," he said. "Every man shall have a bellyful to-day. A stew of these, mixed with dolicho beans—many a ship's company will fare worse than ourselves this day."

I was pleased to find a healthy hunger gnawing at my stomach; nothing could have looked more succulent than the sea food, and every man of us was eager

to be at the camp with the pot set over a good fire.
It was high noon when we joined the others. Peckover's party had just come in with a supply of clams
and oysters almost equal in amount to that in the pot.
They had also found, on the south side of the island,
an abundance of fresh water in hollows of the rocks
—more than enough to fill our vessels. Every circumstance favoured us. The sun shone in a cloudless sky, so that Captain Bligh was able, with his magnifying glass, to kindle a fire at once. The oysters
and clams were now dumped into the pot, together
with a quart and a half of dolicho beans. The
requisite amount of water was added, and to make our
stew yet more tasty, each man's usual amount of bread
was added to it. Smith and Hall, our cooks, had
whittled out long wooden spoons with which they
stirred the stew as it came to a boil, sending up a
savoury steam that made the walls of our empty
bellies quiver with anticipation. When the stew had
cooked for a good twenty minutes,—the time had
seemed hours to most of us,—the pot was set off the
fire; and we gathered round with our half-coconut
shells, while the cooks ladled into each man's shell all
that it could hold of clams, oysters, beans, and delicious broth; and when all had been served, there
was still enough in the pot for a half pint more, all
round. The beans were not so tasty as we had hoped,
but we made a small matter of that.

After our meal we rested for an hour in the shade

of the rocks. I had just fallen into a refreshing sleep when Mr. Bligh aroused me. "Sorry to disturb you, Mr. Ledward," he said, "but we must push on. We are too close to the main here, and I have no desire for any night visits from the savages."

It was then about mid-afternoon. With a light breeze, we directed our course to a group of sandy cays which lay about five leagues off the continental shore. Darkness had fallen before we reached them and, as we could find no suitable landing place, we came to a grapnel and remained in the launch until dawn. All through the night we heard the cries of innumerable sea fowl, and daylight showed us that one of the cays was a place of resort for birds of the noddy kind. We found that we were on the westernmost of four small islands, surrounded by a reef of rocks, and connected with sand banks whose surface was barely above high tide. Within them lay a mirrorlike lagoon with a small passage, into which we brought the launch.

This place, so far from the main, seemed designed by nature as a refuge for men in our condition. Captain Bligh named it "Lagoon Island," and gladdened our hearts by informing us that he proposed to spend the day and the following night here. Unfortunately, the cays were little more than heaps of rock and sand, covered with coarse grass and a sparse growth of bush and stunted trees; but there were enough of these latter to protect us from the heat of the sun.

Our forces were divided so that some could rest while others searched for food. The lagoon abounded in fish; but try as we would, we could catch none. This was a great trial; after repeated unsuccessful efforts, we were forced to fall back upon oysters and clams and the one vegetable which these islands afforded — dolicho beans. Even the shellfish were not abundant here, and the party sent in search of them returned at about ten in the morning with a very small number, so that our dinner this day did little more than aggravate our hunger. During the long voyage from Tofoa we had been so cold and miserable the greater part of the time that the pangs of hunger were kept in check. Furthermore, the constant peril of the sea had prevented us from dwelling upon the thought of food. The case was altered now, and we thought of little else.

After our midday dinner, Elphinstone, with a party of four, was sent to the islet adjoining that at which we lay, to search for sea fowl and their eggs, for we had observed that the birds congregated at that place. The rest of us were glad enough to take our rest, crawling into the shade of bushes and overhanging rocks.

On this afternoon I enjoyed a long and undisturbed sleep which greatly refreshed me; indeed, I did not waken until near sundown, just as Mr. Elphinstone's party was returning. They came in all but empty-handed, having gotten no birds and only three eggs. This was, evidently, not the nesting season: they had found the islet practically deserted; the birds were away fishing for themselves, and the few they had seen were too wary to be caught.

"Nevertheless, we must try again," said Bligh. "They will soon be coming home with full gullets. We can be sure of catching them at night, and there will be a good light from the moon to hunt by. . . . Mr. Cole, you shall try this time. Go warily, mind! Let the birds settle for the night before you go amongst them."

"Aye, sir, we'll see to that," said Cole. Samuel, Tinkler, Lamb, and myself were told off to make up his party; and, having provided ourselves with sticks, we set out for the bird island.

It was a beautiful evening, cool and fresh now that the sun had set. There was not a breath of air stirring, and the surface of the lagoons glowed with the colours of the western sky. Our way led over a causeway of hard-packed sand, laid over the coral reef. It was scarcely a dozen paces across, and curved in a wide arc across a shallow sea filled with mushroom coral that rose to within a few feet of the surface. The bar connecting the islands was about two miles long. Tinkler and Lamb were soon far ahead; the boatswain, Samuel, and I followed at a more leisurely pace, stopping to examine the rock pools

along the reef for clams and oysters, though we
found nothing save a few snails, scarcely larger than
the end of one's thumb. Nevertheless, we gathered
them into the bread bag we had brought to carry
back the birds.

Whilst in Mr. Bligh's company we had been careful
to make no reference to the mutiny. On one occasion, I remember, young Tinkler had ventured to
speak in defense of two of the midshipmen who had
been left behind on the *Bounty;* but Bligh had silenced
him in such a manner that no one else was tempted
to bring up the subject in his presence. But now,
the three of us, freed from restraint, fell naturally
into talk of the seizure of the ship and of what had
led up to it.

"What puzzles me," said Cole, "is that Mr. Christian could have made his plan without any of us
getting wind of it."

"It was a sudden resolve on his part, I am fairly
certain of that," I replied.

"That's my opinion," said Samuel. "No doubt the
villain had plotted it long before, but he bided his
time before opening his mind to the others."

Cole nodded. "Aye, it must have been so," he said.
"What could have brought him to such a mad act,
Mr. Ledward? Can you reason it out? He'd no
better friend than Captain Bligh, and he must have
known it in his heart." He shook his head, wonder-
ingly. "I'd a liking for Mr. Christian," he added.

Samuel stopped short and gazed at the boatswain in a horrified manner.

"'Liking,' Mr. Cole?" he exclaimed.

"Aye," said Cole. "He was hot-tempered and anything but easy under Mr. Bligh's correction; but I never doubted him a gentleman and a loyal officer."

"His Majesty can well spare gentlemen of Christian's kidney from his service," I replied. "You're too lenient in your judgments, Mr. Cole. Whatever else may be said of him, Christian is an intelligent man. He must have known that he was condemning us to all but certain death."

"Begging your pardon, Mr. Ledward, I don't believe he did know it. He must have been out of his mind. . . . This I will say: Mr. Christian will never again know peace. He'll have us on his conscience till the day of his death."

"He'll hang," said Samuel, confidently. "Hide where he may, Captain Bligh will find him and bring him to justice."

"Let that be as it will, Mr. Samuel," said Cole. "I'll warrant he's been punished enough as it is."

"Do you think God could forgive him, Mr. Cole?" I asked, out of curiosity more than for any other reason.

"He could, sir. There's no crime so black that God cannot forgive it if a man truly repents."

"Have *you* forgiven him?" I then asked.

He was silent for a moment as he pondered this question. Then, "No, sir," he replied, firmly. "He shall never have my forgiveness for the wrong he has done Captain Bligh."

We were now close to the bird island. Tinkler alone was awaiting us there.

"Where's Lamb, Mr. Tinkler?" Cole asked. "I told both of you to wait for us."

"He was here a moment ago. I ordered him to help me look for clams while we waited. I'm damned if I know where he's got to."

"It's your *place* to know, Mr. Tinkler," said Samuel shortly. "Captain Bligh shall hear of this if anything goes wrong."

"Now don't be a telltale, Samuel, for God's sake," said Tinkler anxiously. "What did you expect me to do—throw him down and sit on his head? He can't have gone far."

"The man's a fool," said Samuel. "He's not to be trusted out of sight."

"Aye," said Cole, " if there's a wrong way of doing a thing, Lamb will find his way to it. We may as well wait here. There's time enough."

No Lamb appeared, for all our waiting. The afterglow faded from the sky, and the moon, nearing the full, shone with increasing splendour, paling all but the brightest of the stars. The birds must have sensed the presence of enemies, for they were long in settling. They circled in thousands over the is-

land, filling the air with their grating cries, but at
last the deafening clamour died away and we ventured to proceed on our expedition. The island was,
roughly, a mile long and about half as wide, and the
birds appeared to have congregated for the night
on the farthest part of it. We separated to a distance of about fifty yards and had gone but a little
way when the air was again filled with their cries
and the moon all but darkened by their bodies. I
could guess what had happened: the precious Lamb,
without waiting for us, had blundered in amongst
the birds, to the ruin of our plans. I saw Tinkler
and the boatswain break into a run. My own legs
were not equal to the added exertion; indeed, I had so
little strength that I had drawn to the limit of it in
reaching the bird island, and it was all I could now
do to walk, to say nothing of running. By pure
chance I managed to knock down two noddies that
circled low over my head. One of them was only
slightly hurt, and fluttered away from me, but I at
length managed to capture it. Having done so, I
myself fell down, completely exhausted. Shortly
afterward I felt an attack of tenesmus coming on, but
to my surprise and relief I discovered that I was
evacuating, for the first time in thirty-three days.
Perhaps I should pass over this matter in silence; it
is not, under ordinary circumstances, one to be re-
ferred to; but members of my own profession will
understand the interest I took both in the perform-

ance of a function so long delayed, and the result of it. The excrement was something curious to see —hard, round pellets not so large as sheep's turds, and looking perfectly black in the moonlight. The amount was woefully small, and yet I believe that it was all my bowels contained at that time. It confirmed me in the opinion I had ventured to Mr. Nelson—that our bodies had absorbed all but an infinitesimal amount of the little nourishment they had received.

With my two precious birds, I now walked feebly on after my companions, whom I at length found in one spot, gathered around the crouching form of the recreant Lamb.

"Look at this wretch, Mr. Ledward!" Samuel shouted, his voice trembling with rage. "Do you see what he has done?"

Cole said nothing, but stood with his arms folded, gazing at the man. Overhead, the noddies circled about in thousands; but they were far beyond reach. Their cries were all but deafening; we had to shout to make ourselves heard.

But no words were needed to tell me the tale of what had happened. Lamb's face and hands were smeared with blood, and around him lay the gnawed carcasses of nine birds which he had caught and devoured. I must do him the credit to say that he had made a good job of them; scarcely anything remained but feathers, bones, and entrails. He was making some whining appeal that could not be heard above the tumult of birds' cries. Of a sudden the boatswain gave him a cuff that knocked him sprawling at full length in the sand. Then Mr. Cole bent over him. "Stop here!" he roared. "If you move from this spot, you rogue, I 'll thrash you within an inch of your life!"

We continued a quest that was now all but hopeless. The birds were thoroughly alarmed, and although we waited for a full two hours, they would not again settle. A few ventured down, but before we could reach them they would take wing again. We caught but twelve in all, though we should have returned with our bag filled.

We trudged back slowly, worn out with the fatigue of the journey and reluctant to reach our camp, for we well knew how bitter would be the disappointment of those awaiting our return. This was the first bird island we had met with, and we had looked forward to a meal of roasted sea fowl with an expectation that might have been laughable had it not been so pathetic.

Mr. Cole carried the bag, driving Lamb on before him. The man persisted in his abject entreaties, begging that nothing be said of the matter to Mr. Bligh: —

"I was out o' me head, Mr. Cole. I was, straight. I was that starved —"

"Starved?" said Samuel. "And what of the rest

of us, you bloody thief? Out of your head! You can tell that to Captain Bligh!"

The boatswain halted. "Mr. Samuel, we'd best not let him know the whole truth of it."

"What?" exclaimed Samuel. "Would you shield such a villain? When he's robbed some of us, it may be, of the very chance of life?"

"It's not that I'd shield him," said Cole, "but I'd be ashamed to let Captain Bligh know what a poor thing we've got amongst us."

"He knows already," Samuel replied. "Hasn't the man been a dead weight to us all the way from Tofoa? He's done nothing but lie and whine in the bottom of the boat all the voyage. We've him to thank, I'll be bound, for the stolen pork!"

"I didn't touch it, sir! I didn't!"

"You did, you rogue! It must have been you! There's none but yourself would have been such a cur as to steal from his shipmates!"

He was, in all truth, a wretched creature, the inestimable Lamb. I have little doubt that Samuel was right in surmising that he was the thief of the pork. But as that was gone, and the birds as well, I agreed with Cole that nothing was to be gained by disclosing Lamb's gorge of raw bird flesh. Tinkler sided with us, and Samuel at length agreed to keep that point a secret.

"But Captain Bligh shall know whose fault it was that the birds were frightened," he said.

"Aye," said Cole. "We owe it to ourselves that that should be told." And so it was agreed.

Captain Bligh was, of course, furious. He took the man's bird stick and thrashed him soundly with it; and never was punishment more richly deserved.

We were a sad company that evening. A fire of coals had been carefully tended against our return, when the fowls were to be roasted, and every man had promised himself at least two of the birds. But when Mr. Bligh saw the miserable result of our expedition, although the twelve birds were dressed and cooked, they were carefully packed away for future use; and we had for supper water, the handful of sea snails we had found, and a few oysters. Elphinstone and Hayward were then set at watch, and the rest of us lay down to sleep.

It seemed to me that I had no more than closed my eyes when I was aroused to find the island in a glare of light. The night was chill and the master had kindled a fire for himself at a distance from the rest of us. Some coarse dry grass which covered the island had caught from this, and the fire spread rapidly, burning fiercely for a time. It was the last straw for Mr. Bligh. We made a vain effort to beat out the flames, and when at last they had burned themselves out, he gave the company in general, and Mr. Fryer in particular, a dressing down that lasted for the better part of a quarter of an hour.

"You, sir," he roared at Fryer, "who should set

an example with myself to all the rest, are a disgrace to your calling! You are the most incompetent bloody rascal of the company! Mark my words! We 'll have the savages on us as a result of this! And serve you right if we do! What are you worth, the lot of you? A more useless set of rogues it has never been my misfortune to command! I send you out for birds, to an island where they congregate in thousands. You frighten them like a lot of children, and get none. I send you out for shellfish. You get none. I set you to fishing. You get none. And yet you expect me to feed you! And if I close my eyes for ten minutes, you 're up to some deviltry that may be the ruination of us all! And you expect me to take you safe to Timor! By God, if I do, it will be thanks to none of you!"

He quieted down presently. "Get you to sleep," he said gruffly. "This may be our last night ashore till the end of the voyage, so make the most of it."

I lay awake for some time. Nelson, who was lying beside me, turned presently to whisper in my ear.

"What a man he is, Ledward," he said. "It comforted me to see him in a passion again. We'll fetch Timor. I did him a great injustice ever to doubt it."

I had precisely the same feeling, and I thanked God, inwardly, that Bligh and no other was in command of the *Bounty*'s launch.

CHAPTER XI

WE were astir before daylight, greatly refreshed by six or seven hours of sleep. Mr. Bligh awoke in the best of humours, intending to embark immediately, but was irritated when he found that Lamb was too ill to go into the launch.

"What ails the fellow, Mr. Ledward?" he asked, looking down at the man with an expression of disgust.

Lamb was doubled up with cramps from his gorge of the night before; there was no doubting the pain he suffered. I was tempted to let Bligh know the truth of the matter, for my impatience with this worse than useless fellow was equal to his own. I refrained, however, and was about to purge him when he was seized with a violent flux. Half an hour later he was carried into the boat and we proceeded on our way.

It was a beautiful morning, with cloudless sky, and a fresh breeze at E.S.E. This part of the coast of New Holland lies, as our sailors would say, "in the eye of the southeast trades"; and during the time we sailed within the reefs we had constantly a fine, fresh sailing breeze abaft the beam.

Mr. Fryer was at the tiller. Captain Bligh sat beside him with his journal open on his knees, engaged in his usual occupation of charting the coast. He glanced frequently at the compass to obtain bearings on the points, indentations and landmarks ashore; at short intervals, without raising his eyes from his work, he would order "Heave the log," and make a note of the launch's speed. Nelson had told me, what I could readily believe, that Captain Cook, in spite of Bligh's youth at that time, considered him among the most skilled cartographers in England. And I am confident that the officer who will one day be appointed to make a thorough survey of this coast will be amazed at the accuracy of Bligh's chart, drawn with only his sextant, a compass, and a rude log to aid him, in the stern sheets of a twenty-three-foot boat, sailing fast to the north with scarcely a halt.

All the time we sailed within the reefs of New Holland, Bligh was absorbed in this work, to such an extent that for hours at a time he seemed to forget our very presence. Mr. Bligh was an explorer born, but his interest was less in the strange people and natural curiosities to be found than in the charting of new coasts. I feel assured that there were entire hours within the reefs when he forgot the *Bounty*, forgot the mutiny, forgot that he was in a small unarmed boat, half starved, at the mercy of savage tribes, and hundreds of leagues from the nearest European settlement. His expression of interest and happiness at these times was such that it was a pleasure merely to look at his face.

We had sailed about two leagues to the northward when a heavy swell began to set in from the east, leading us to suppose that there must be a break in the reefs which protect most of this shore. The sea continued rough as we passed between a shoal, on which were two sandy cays, and two other islets four miles to the west. Toward midday we sailed past six other cays covered with fresh green scrub and contrasting with the main, which now appeared barren, with sand hills along the coast. A flat-topped hill abreast of us, Captain Bligh named "Pudding-Pan Hill"; and two rounded hills, a little to the north, he called "The Paps." At two hours before sunset we passed a large inlet, which Bligh longed to explore. It appeared to be the entrance to a safe and commodious harbour.

Three leagues to the northward of this inlet, we found a small island where we decided to spend the night. The sea was rough, the wind was now making up in gusts, and there was a strong current setting to the north. Though well wooded, with low scrub, the island appeared the merest pile of rocks, with only one poor landing place in the lee of a point. A shark of monstrous proportions swam alongside the boat for some time while we approached the land, and as we rounded the point, some of the people saw a large animal resembling a crocodile pass under the boat.

"Bigger'n the launch, he was," said Cole when the captain questioned him; "with four legs and a great long tail. A crocodile, ye can lay to that, sir."

It was a wretched anchorage, for the coral dropped in a vertical wall from the surface to a depth of two fathoms, and the bottom was very foul. The wind was making up, and the current swept in fast around the point.

Laying the boat alongside the rocks, Captain Bligh ordered Fryer and some of the people to spend the night on shore, since the anchorage was too uncertain for all to leave the boat in such weather. As we drifted fast to leeward, the grapnel was dropped. It dragged for a moment, and presently held as scope was paid out; then, as the weight of the launch fetched up against it, the line parted suddenly.

"Enough scope, you fools!" roared Bligh, not knowing what had happened. "Damn you, boatswain! What are you about, there?"

"We've lost the grapnel, sir!" Cole shouted.

"To the oars!"

The men ran out their oars and pulled with a will, for they realized as well as the captain the dangers of being blown offshore on such a night. Their utmost exertions were just sufficient to gain slowly against current and wind. Bligh made his way forward where Cole was examining the broken line.

"A rotten spot, sir," said the boatswain; "the rust

of the grapnel did it." He opened his clasp knife and cut away the rotten line.

Bligh was peering down into the water ahead. "Hold her here!" he ordered without turning his head.

There was something ominous about the place, and the wild red sunset; the thought of the monsters we had seen so short a time before would have deterred most men from doing what Bligh now did. He stripped off his ragged shirt and trousers, seized the end of the grapnel line, and plunged into the sea.

Cole gazed after him anxiously; then, seeing that the people had stopped rowing for a moment in their astonishment, he roared out: —

"Pull, I say! Do you want to drag the line out of the captain's hands? Pull, damn your blood!"

He was paying out line as he shouted, and gazing earnestly down into the water. Captain Bligh came to the surface, drew three or four long breaths, and dived once more. Nearly a minute passed before he reappeared. This time he swam to the stern of the boat and pulled himself aboard. For a moment or two he sat on the gunwale, breathing rapidly.

"By God, sir," I remarked. "I'm glad you did not ask *me* to dive."

He laughed grimly. "I was none too eager to go down; but I'll ask no one to do what I fear to do myself. The thought of the monstrous shark was never out of my mind." He shivered. "Nelson, what was that other thing we saw—a crocodile?"

"I've little doubt of it," Nelson replied. "Captain Cook saw what he believed were crocodiles in these waters."

Bligh shivered in spite of himself. "I'm as glad to be in the boat again." he said. "We are in a bad position here, and these currents are the devil; they seem to set four ways at once."

"You were fortunate to get down to the grapnel, sir," said Peckover.

"Aye, Mr. Peckover, the Indians of Otaheite are the men for that work. I managed to get the line roved through its ring before I had to come up to blow; but one of them would have stopped down to bend it on. We whites are good for nothing under water."

Dusk was setting in, and we profited by what remained of daylight to eat our small portions of the half-dressed birds left over from those obtained on Lagoon Island. In the strong wind and current, the boat rode uneasily to her grapnel, and we passed a wretched night. The moon, close on to the full, set sometime before daylight; in the first gray of dawn, Captain Bligh and some of the rest of us landed to see what we could obtain on shore, leaving Cole and Peckover in charge of the launch.

Nelson had passed a pretty comfortable night in the lee of some rocks; I found him awake, and he and I set out to explore the far side of the island. As we crossed through the scrub, we found the backs of many turtles, some of great size, and the fireplaces where the Indians had roasted the flesh. I was engaged in a futile search for clams on a small, sandy beach exposed to the east wind, when I heard Nelson shout.

I swung about, and saw him trying to turn over a turtle of immense size, which had just emerged from behind some bushes and was making her way to the water's edge.

"*Ledward!*" he shouted again, in an agonized voice.

In an instant I was at his side, but our combined strength was not enough to raise one side of the turtle from the sand. All the time we struggled to turn her, she was plying her flippers desperately, sending showers of sand over us and moving rapidly toward the sea, only a few yards distant. Her strength was prodigious; she must have weighed not less than four hundred pounds. Perceiving the impossibility of turning her, we gave up the attempt, and seized a hind flipper each, holding back with all our might. But she had reached the damp sand by now, where her powerful fore flippers could obtain a hold, and in spite of our utmost exertions she dragged us, little by little, into the sea. Through the shallows she went, while our grips weakened; then suddenly, as she plunged into deep water, we were forced to let go.

Panting, and wet from head to foot, we had barely the strength to make our way back to the sand. Once there, we sank down side by side. After a long silence Nelson looked up at me with a wry smile.

"By God!" he said sadly. "That was tragedy! There was a fortnight's food in the beast, Ledward!"

"All of that," I replied. "She may have laid some eggs. Let us go and search."

Nelson shook his head. "No. I surprised her as she was beginning to dig. She had just come up from the sea, for her back was still wet."

We fell silent once more, and at last he said: "We'll say nothing of this to the others, eh, Ledward?"

We walked slowly back across the island, halting on a bit of rising ground to rest. A little to the left we could see the others gathered on the beach near the launch. Nelson lay back for a moment, his hands behind his head, and stretched out his legs at full length.

"You'd best follow my example," he said. "It may be the last chance we shall have."

"The last? Surely not!" I exclaimed.

"Bligh thinks we shall be clear of the coast by to-morrow or the day after."

I managed to smile somewhat dubiously. "Between ourselves, Nelson, I'll confess that no man in the boat can dread the prospect more than I."

"Dread it? I positively quake at the thought! God help us if we have any more nights like those on the way to New Holland!"

We found Bligh awaiting us. The others had obtained nothing, so he hailed the launch, and we soon set sail. The main at this place bore from S.E. to N.N.W. half W., and a high, flat-topped island lay to the north, four or five leagues distant.

On passing this island, we found a great opening in the coast, set with a number of mountainous islands. To the north and west the country was high, wooded, and broken, with many islands close in with the land. We were now steering more and more to the west, and Captain Bligh informed us that he was tolerably certain we should be clear of the coast of New Holland in the course of the afternoon.

Toward two o'clock, as we were steering toward the westernmost part of the main now in sight, we fell in with a vast sandy shoal which extends out many miles to sea, and were obliged to haul our wind to weather it. Bligh named the place "Shoal Cape." Just before dark we passed a small island, or rock, on which innumerable boobies were roosting. There was no land in sight to the north, south, or west.

Three hundred leagues of empty sea now lay between us and Timor.

The six days we had spent within the reefs of New Holland had allowed us to sleep in some comfort at night, and to refresh ourselves with what little the islands afforded. And, above all, the barriers of coral shielded us from the attacks of our old enemy, the sea.

But the sea had not forgotten us, and lay in wait, on the far side of Shoal Cape, armed with strong gales from the east and deluges of rain, unabated for seven days. On the misery of that week I shall not dwell.

On the morning of June tenth, I was lying doubled up in the stern sheets. Lamb, Simpson, and Nelson were in a state as bad as my own; and Lebogue, the *Bounty's* sailmaker, once the hardiest of old seamen, lay forward with closed eyes. His legs were swollen in a shocking manner, and his flesh had lost its elasticity; when it was pinched or squeezed, the impression of one's fingers remained clear.

The breeze was still fresh, though the sea had moderated during the night, and only two men were at the bails. Elphinstone was steering, with Bligh at his side. The countenances of both men looked hollow as those of spectres; but while the master's mate stared at the compass dully, the captain's eyes were calm. Our fishing line was made fast close behind Bligh. We had towed it constantly, day and night, for more than three thousand miles without catching a fish, though Cole and Peckover had exhausted their ingenuity in devising a variety of lures made from feathers and rags. Peckover had seized a new one on our hook the night before, employing the feathers of a booby Captain Bligh had caught with his own hands on the fifth—the only bird we had secured since leaving New Holland.

Bemused with weakness, I happened to glance at

the line. We were sailing at not less than four knots at the time, and I was surprised to observe that the line, instead of towing behind us, ran out at right angles to the boat. For a moment I did not realize the significance of this. Then I said, in the best voice I could muster: "A fish!"

Mr. Bligh started, seized the line, rose to his feet, and began to haul in hand-over-hand, with a strength that surprised me.

"By God, lads," he exclaimed, "this one shan't get away!"

It was a dolphin of about twenty pounds' weight. The captain brought it in leaping and splashing, swung it over the gunwale, and fell to the floor boards, clasping it to his chest.

"Your knife, Mr. Peckover!" he called, never for an instant relaxing his hold on the struggling fish.

In an instant the gunner had cut the cord beneath the gills, but Mr. Bligh held fast to the dolphin while it blazed with the changing colours of death and its shuddering grew weaker, till it lay still and limp. The captain rose weakly, rinsed his hands over the side, and sat down once more, breathing fast. Peckover looked at him admiringly.

"No use his trying them jumping-jack tricks on you, sir!" he said.

"You've Mr. Ledward to thank," said Bligh. "We've towed so long without luck, that I'll be bound no other man would have noticed it!"

Peckover was gazing down longingly at the bulging side of the fish, and Bligh went on: "Aye, divide him up — guts, liver, and all."

Peckover knelt beside the fish, muttering to himself as he laid out imaginary lines of division, and then changed his mind. At last he began to cut. The people watched this operation with an eagerness which might have been laughable under happier circumstances. Only Elphinstone, at the tiller, had preserved an attitude of indifference throughout the affair, gazing vacantly at the compass and up at the horizon from time to time.

Under Bligh's direction, the gunner divided the fish into thirty-six shares, each of about half a pound. Eighteen of these were now distributed by our method of "Who shall have this?" A fine steak fell to me; the captain got the liver and about two ounces of flesh. Lebogue shook his head feebly when his share was offered him, and whispered: "I'm past eatin', lad."

I managed to turn on my side when Tinkler handed me my fish in a coconut shell, but I was now in such a state that the sight of raw flesh revolted my stomach. Seeing that Nelson felt the same, I did my best to make a pretense of eating before stowing my shell away out of sight. I am not of a rugged constitution, and it irked me to be so feeble when others were still able to bail and work the sails. Nelson was close beside me, and he said in a low voice: "Damme, Ledward, I cannot eat the fish."

"Nor I," I replied.

"No matter, we'll soon raise Timor."

"Mr. Samuel," said Bligh, "issue a spoonful of wine to those who are weakest."

He was eating the dolphin's liver, and I could see that he relished the food no more than I. But he forced himself sternly, mouthful by mouthful, to chew and swallow it.

Toward noon, the wind shifted from E.S.E. to nearly northeast, forcing us to lower our sails and raise them on the starboard tack. Then a black rain squall bore down on us, filling our kegs and permitting us to drink our fill. Those who were able wrung out their sodden rags in salt water, and performed the same office for their weaker mates. The sky was clouded over, and though there was a long swell from the east, the wind was light and we shipped little water over the stern. The boatswain was staring aft.

"Look, sir!" he exclaimed suddenly to Bligh.

Several of the people turned their heads; as I raised myself a little to look, I heard Hallet say: "What's that?"

Directly in our wake and not more than a quarter of a mile away, a black cloud hung low over the sea, with a sagging point that approached the water in a curious, jerking fashion. And just beneath, the surface of the sea was agitated as if by a small maelstrom. Little by little, the sea rose in a conical point, making a rushing, roaring noise that was now plainly audible; little by little, the cloud sagged down to meet it.

Then suddenly the sea and cloud met in a whirling column which lengthened as the cloud above seemed to rise rapidly.

"Only a waterspout," said Bligh, after a glance aft. "Look alive, if I give the word."

For a time it seemed to remain stationary, growing taller and thicker as if gathering its force. Then it began to move, bearing straight down on us.

"Bear up," Bligh ordered the helmsman quietly. "Aye, so!" And, as the sails began to slat, "To the sheets, lads! Trim them flat!"

We changed our course not a moment too soon. The cloud, now overhead, was as black as ink, with a kind of greenish pallor at its heart; we had not sailed fifty yards, close-hauled, when the waterspout passed astern of us, a sight of awe-inspiring majesty.

All hands save Mr. Bligh stared at it in silent consternation. The column of water, many hundreds of feet high and thicker than the greatest oak in England, had a clear, glassy look and seemed to revolve with incredible rapidity. At its base, the sea churned and roared with a sound that would have made a loud shout inaudible. I doubt if any man in the boat was greatly afraid; we had gone through so much, and were so reduced by our sufferings, that death had become a matter of little moment. But even in my own state of weakness, I trembled in awe at this manifestation of God's majesty upon the deep. Not a word was spoken till the waterspout was half a mile distant and Bligh ordered the course changed once more.

"Ledward," remarked Nelson coolly, in a weak voice, "I wouldn't have missed that for a thousand pounds!"

"I have seen many of them," said Bligh, "though never so close. There's little danger, save at night . . ."

He shut his mouth suddenly and bent double in a spasm of pain. Next moment his head was over the gunwale while he retched and vomited. After a long time he rinsed his mouth with sea water, and sat up ghastly pale.

"Some water, Mr. Samuel," he managed to say. "Aye, a full half pint."

The water sent him to the gunwale once more, and during the remainder of the afternoon Mr. Bligh was in a pitiable state. I believe that the liver of the dolphin must have been poisonous, as is said often to be the case; though it may be that Bligh had reached the state I was in, in which the exhausted stomach can no longer accept food. Though constantly retching and vomiting, and suffering from excruciating cramps, he refused to lie down; he kept an eye on our course between his paroxysms, and directed the trimming of the sails. At sunset he took a spoonful of wine, which his stomach retained, and seemed better for it.

Though I no longer felt hunger or much pain, the night seemed interminably long. The moon came up

at about ten o'clock, dead astern of us, and shone full
in my face. I dozed, awoke, attempted to stretch
my cramped legs, and dozed again. Sometimes I
heard Nelson muttering in his sleep. The captain
managed to doze for a time in the early hours of the
night; when the moon was about two hours up, he
relieved Fryer at the helm. The moon was at its
zenith, from which I judged the time to be four in
the morning, when Bligh roused Elphinstone, and
again lay down to sleep. The wind was at east, and
though the moonlight paled the stars, I could see the
Southern Cross on our larboard beam.

I had said nothing to the others of my fears, but
for a day or two past I had had reason to suspect that
Elphinstone's mind was giving way under the strain.
He was as little wasted in body as any man in the
launch, yet his vacant eye, his lack of interest in what
went on about him, and his strange gestures and mut-
terings were symptoms of a failing mind, although
there was no reason to think him unequal to his duties.
When Bligh took him by the shoulder to waken him,
he said "Aye, sir!" in a dull voice, and took the tiller
mechanically.

It was Peckover's watch; turning my head, I could
see him seated with some others forward. His shoulders were bowed, and from time to time he nodded
and caught himself, making heroic efforts to stay
awake. A continual sound of faint groans and mut-
terings came from the men asleep in the bottom of

the launch; dreamless sleep had been unknown to us for many days. Soon Bligh began to snore gently and irregularly.

Elphinstone sat motionless at the tiller, staring ahead with a vacant expression on his face. I could see his lips move as he muttered to himself, but could hear no sound. Then for a time I dozed.

It was still night when I awoke, though close to dawn. The master's mate was hunched at the helm, seeming scarcely to have moved since I glanced at him last. For a time I noticed nothing out of the way; then, looking over the gunwale, I perceived that the Cross was no longer on our beam. It was on the larboard bow; our course had been changed from west to southwest. Elphinstone leaned toward me.

"The land!" he whispered eagerly. "Yonder, dead ahead! Take care! Don't waken Mr. Bligh!"

I struggled with some difficulty into a position which enabled me to look forward. Peckover and the others sat sleeping, bowed on the thwarts. Ahead of the launch was only the vast moonlit sea, and an horizon empty save for a few scattered clouds.

"Timor," whispered Elphinstone, triumphantly. "God's with us, Mr. Ledward! He caused the wind to shift to the northeast, so we're dead before it still. You see it now, eh? The mountains and the great valleys? A fine island, I'll be bound, where we'll find all we need!"

He spoke with such sincerity that I looked ahead

once more, beginning to doubt my own eyes; but I saw only the roll of the empty sea under the moon. Bligh stirred and struggled to a sitting position. He took in the situation at a glance.

"What's this, Mr. Elphinstone?" he said in a harsh voice. "Who ordered you to change the course?"

"The land, Captain Bligh! Look ahead! I steered for it when I sighted the mountains an hour ago."

Bligh swung about to stare over the sea. "Land?" he said, as if doubting the evidence of his own senses. "Where?"

"Dead ahead, sir. Can't you see the great valley yonder, and the high ridge above? It looks an island as rich as Otaheite!"

Bligh gave me a quick glance. "Go forward, Mr. Elphinstone," he ordered. "Lie down at once and get some sleep."

To my surprise, the master's mate said no more about the land, but gave the tiller to Bligh and made his way forward amongst the sleeping men. His face wore the mild, vacant expression of a man walking in his sleep.

"Mr. Peckover!" called Bligh harshly.

The gunner started a little and straightened his back slowly. "Aye, aye, sir!" he said.

"Don't let me catch you sleeping on watch again! You and those with you might have been the ruin of us all!" The other members of the watch were stirring, and the captain went on: "I'm going to wear.

To the halyards! Get her on the starboard tack!"

When the halyards had been slacked away and the gaffs of our lugsails passed around to the larboard sides of the masts, Bligh bore up to the west, and the men trimmed the sails to the northeast wind.

This day, the eleventh of June, seemed the longest of my life. They had eaten the last of the dolphin the night before, and at sunrise a quarter of a pint of water and our usual allowance of bread were issued. I drank the water, but could not eat the bread. The captain made a grimace in spite of himself as he raised his morsel of bread to his mouth, but he munched it heroically, nevertheless, and contrived to keep it down. The boatswain had administered a spoonful of wine to Lebogue, and was coming to do the like for Nelson and me. Stepping over the after thwart with the bottle in his hand, he came face to face with Bligh, while an expression of horror came into his eyes.

"Sir," he said solicitously, "ye look worse'n any man in the launch. Ye'd best have a drop o' this."

Bligh smiled at the old fellow's simplicity, and said: "I'll pay you a handsomer compliment, Mr. Cole: you have lasted better than many of the younger men. . . . No, no wine for me. There are those who need it more."

Cole touched his forelock and turned to serve me, shaking his head.

I lay half dozing whilst the sun crawled interminably toward the zenith. Sometimes I opened my eyes after what seemed the passage of hours, only to discover that the shadow of the helmsman had shortened by no more than an inch. My whole life, up to the time we had left Tofoa, seemed but an instant beside the eternity I had spent in the boat, and on this day, after a long process of slowing down, I felt that time had come to a halt at last: I had always been sailing west before a fresh easterly breeze, with the sun stationary and low behind the launch, and would sail thus forever and ever, on a limitless plain of tossing blue, unbroken by any land. And Mr. Bligh would always hold the tiller — a scarecrow clad in grotesque rags, with a turban made of an old pair of trousers on his head.

Noon came at last, and Cole took the tiller while the master and Peckover held Bligh up to take the altitude of the sun. Owing to his own weakness and that of the men supporting him, he had difficulty in getting his sight; though not breaking, the sea was confused, and the launch tossed and pitched uncertainly. After some time, he handed his sextant to the master and sat down to work out our position. Finally he looked up.

"Our latitude is nine degrees, forty-one minutes south," he said; "that of the middle portion of Timor. By my reckoning, we have traversed thirteen and one-half degrees of longitude since leaving Shoal Cape,

—more than eight hundred miles,—and to the best of my recollection the most easterly part of Timor is laid down in one hundred and twenty-eight degrees east longitude, a meridian we must have passed."

"When shall we raise the land, sir?" the boatswain asked.

"During the night or early in the morning. We must keep a sharp lookout to-night."

Toward sunset, when I awoke from a long doze, there were great numbers of sea birds about. Lying on my back, I could see them passing and repassing overhead. Tinkler contrived to strike down one booby with the spare gaff we had cut at Restoration Island, but the others took warning at this and avoided the boat. The bird was reserved for the next day, but I was offered a wineglass of its blood, which I managed to swallow only to vomit it up instantly. There was much rockweed around us, and coconut husks so fresh that they were still bright yellow in colour.

Darkness came, and still the wind held steady and fair. Every man able to sit up was on the thwarts, staring out over the tossing sea ahead, dimly visible in the light of the stars.

Like a sentient being, aware that the end of her long journey was at hand, the launch now seemed to surpass herself. With all sail set and drawing, she raced westward, shipping so little water that there was little need to bail. Sometimes the people were

silent; sometimes I heard them speaking in low tones.
I was aware of an undercurrent of new courage and
confidence, of deep contentment that our trials were
so nearly at an end.   Not once during the long voyage had their faith in Mr. Bligh waned; he had de-
clared that we should raise the land by morning, and
that was enough.

It must have been nearly eleven o'clock when the
moon rose, directly astern of the launch: a bright
half-moon, sailing a cloudless sky.   Hour after hour,
as the moon climbed the heavens, the launch ran
westward, whilst we listened to the crisp sound of
water rushing under her keel.

Even old Lebogue revived a little at this time.
No man of us had endured more grievous suffering,
and yet he had borne his part in the work when
others no weaker than himself lay helpless.

Bligh had taken the tiller at midnight, after an
attempt to sleep; and toward three in the morning,
when the moon was high above the horizon astern,
young Tinkler stepped up on to the after thwart to
peer ahead.   He stood there for some time, swaying to
the motion of the boat, with hands cupped above his
eyes.   Then he sprang down to face the captain.

"The land, sir!" he exclaimed in a shaking voice.

Bligh motioned Fryer to take the helm, and stood
up.   I heard a burst of talk forward: "Only a cloud!"
"No, no!   Land, and high land too!"   Then, as the
launch reared high on a swell, we saw the shadowy

outlines of the land ahead: pale, lofty, and unsubstantial in the light of the moon, a great island still many miles distant, stretching far away to the northeast and southwest. The captain stared ahead long and earnestly before he spoke.

"Timor, lads!" he said.

CHAPTER XII

THERE were some who doubted the landfall, who could not believe that the goal of our voyage was actually in sight. For all Mr. Bligh's quiet assurance, and the boatswain's repeated "Aye, lad! There's the land—never a doubt of it!" they dared not believe, lest day should come and the dim outlines melt into the shapes of distant clouds. We hauled on a wind to the northeast, and those who could stood on the thwarts from time to time, their confidence in what they saw increasing from moment to moment. Some could do no more than raise themselves to a sitting position in the bottom of the launch, clinging to the thwarts or to the gunwales as they stared ahead.

Veil after veil of moonlit obscurity was drawn aside, and at last, in the clear light of early dawn, there it lay: Paradise itself, it seemed, its lofty outlines filling half the circle of the horizon, bearing from S.W. to N.E. by E. The sun rose, its shafts of level, golden light striking across promontory after promontory. We saw great valleys filled with purple shadow, and, high above the coast, forests appeared, interspersed with glades and lawns that might well have been the haunts where our first parents wandered in the innocence of the world.

Our capacities for joy and gratitude were not adequate to the occasion. Mr. Bligh, was, I believe, as near to tears as he had ever been in his life, but he held himself well under control. Others gave way to their emotion, and wept freely; indeed, we were so weak that tears came readily. Poor Elphinstone, alone of our company, was robbed of the joy of that never-to-be-forgotten morning; his sufferings had deprived him — temporarily, at least — of reason. He sat amidships, facing aft, scanning the empty sea behind us with an expression of hopeless bewilderment, an object of commiseration to all. Despite our efforts, we could not convince him that the land lay close ahead.

At the sunrise we were within two leagues of the coast. A land more green and fair has never gladdened seamen's eyes; scarcely a man of us did not long to go ashore at once. The coast was low, but on the higher regions beyond, we saw many cultivated spots. Near one of the plantations we observed several huts, but no people there or elsewhere. Purcell and the master ventured to suggest to Mr. Bligh that we land, in hopes of finding some of the inhabitants, who might inform us as to the whereabouts of the Dutch settlement.

"I can well understand your impatience, Mr.

Fryer," said Bligh; "but we shall take no unnecessary risks. If my recollection serves me, Timor is all of one hundred leagues in extent. I have told you that I am by no means certain that the Dutch have a permanent outpost here. If they have, they may have subjected only a small part of the island to their rule. The inhabitants are, I believe, Malays, well known to be a cruel and treacherous race. We shall place ourselves in their power only as a last resort."

There was no disputing the wisdom of this decision. What we feared, of course, was that no European settlement existed on the island; but we did not permit ourselves to consider this melancholy possibility, and both Bligh and Nelson recollected that Captain Cook had been informed that the most easterly station of the Dutch was upon Timor.

We bore away again to the W.S.W., keeping close enough to the coast to avoid missing any opening that might exist; but throughout the morning neither cover nor bay did we see, nor any place where a landing might have been effected, because of the great surf breaking all along this windward shore.

At noon we were abreast of a high headland only three miles distant, and, having found it, we found the land still bearing off in a southwesterly direction for as far as the eye could reach. Our dinner was the usual allowance: one twenty-fifth of a pound of bread, and a half pint of water — for Mr. Bligh was

not the man to relax his vigilance until assured that
the need for vigilance was past; but the bird we had
caught the night before was divided in the customary
manner. I received a portion of the breast, which, a
week earlier, I should have considered a tidbit of the
rarest sort; but now my stomach revolted at the
sight and tainted smell of the raw flesh, and I could
not eat it. I gave my portion to Peckover, and
merely to see the relish with which he devoured it up-
set me the more, so that I fell to retching violently.
Six or seven others were in as bad a state. Mr. Bligh
gave the weakest of us a swallow of rum, of which
we still had three quarters of a bottle.

All through the afternoon the weather was hazy,
and we could see no great distance before us, but
were close enough in to observe the appearance of the
coast, which was low and covered with a seemingly
endless forest of fan palms. At this time we saw no
signs anywhere of cultivated spots, and, as we proceeded, the land had a more arid look. Captain
Bligh said nothing of the matter; but I could see that
he was worried lest we had gone beyond the habitable
part of the island. I know not how many times
during this day we had before us a distant promontory, beyond which nothing of the island could be
seen; but always, upon rounding it, we found another
far ahead, and the land still bearing away to the
south. At sunset, we had run twenty-three miles
since noon; and in the gathering dusk we brought to

under a close-reefed foresail, in shoal water within half a league of the shore.

We did not know how near we might be to the end of all our troubles. Perhaps only a few miles farther, we thought, lay the Dutch settlement; but we dared not risk sailing on, lest we should run past it in the darkness. The excitement of the previous eighteen hours had exhausted our little strength, and, had it been possible, I believe that Captain Bligh would have landed here, if only to give us the refreshment of stretching out our cramped and aching limbs. The surf on shore was not great at this point, but we were too weak to have run our boat through it; so we lay huddled in the launch, most of us too far spent even for conversation. In my own case, much as I regret to admit it, I was in a weaker condition than any of the company save Lebogue, and I had a great ulcer on my leg that kept me in constant torment. We were all of us, in fact, covered with sores, due to the constant chafing of our emaciated bodies against the boards of the boat, and kept open and raw by the action of salt water. Nelson astonished me at this time; he looked like a dying man, but he seemed to have drawn, merely from the sight of Timor, a strength which he was, somehow, able to impart to others. Together, he and Bligh took over the office of looking after the sick, and I shall not soon forget their comforting, heartening words as they made their way amongst us, helping some poor fellow to change to a more comfortable position, and doling out a few drops of rum or wine from the last of our precious supply.

We were drawn together that night as never before. We had suffered so much that we seemed of one body. Antipathies, whether small or large, arising from our different characters, vanished quite away, and a rich current of sympathy and common feeling ran through our forlorn little company, making us, for that night at least, brothers indeed. I had observed many different aspects of Mr. Bligh's character, and, profoundly as I respected him, I had not supposed that he had in him any deep feeling of compassion for the men under his command. On this occasion he revealed a gentleness which quite altered my conception of his nature. The experience brought home to me the difficulty one has in forming a true notion of any of one's fellow creatures. They must be seen over a long period of time, and under many and varied conditions not often presenting themselves in sequence to a single observer. But some men are ever the same, unchanging and unchangeable as rock, no matter what the conditions. Cole, the boatswain, was one of these. Loyalty to his commander, devotion to duty, sympathy for those weaker than himself, and an abiding trust in God were the corner stones of his nature. All through that interminable night he was ever on the alert to do some suffering man a kindness.

About two in the morning, we wore and stood close along the coast till daylight. Seeing no signs of habitation, we bore away to the westward, with a strong gale against a weather current, which occasioned much sea and forced us to resume the weary work of bailing. This fell chiefly upon Fryer, Cole, Peckover, and two of the midshipmen, Tinkler and Hayward; others did what little they could, sitting propped up against the thwarts.

By this time every man of us—save Bligh, perhaps—had a feeling of mingled fear and hatred toward the sea: as though it were not a mindless force but a conscious one, bent upon our destruction, and becoming increasingly enraged that we had survived its cruelty and were about to escape. Even Bligh must have had something of the feeling, for I heard him say to the master: "She's not done with us yet. . . . Bail, lads!" he called. "I'll soon have you out of this."

Once more we had before us a low coast, with points opening to the west; and again we were encouraged to think we had reached the extremity of the island; but, toward the middle of the morning, we found the coast reaching on to the south a weary way ahead. Even the land, to my distorted fancy, appeared hostile—unwilling to receive us, tempting us on with false hopes only that we might be the more bitterly disappointed.

Presently we discerned, to the southwest, the dim

outlines of high land, but in the moisture-laden air we could not be sure whether or no it was a part of Timor. Seeing no break between it and the coast we were following, Bligh concluded that it must be a distant headland of the island; therefore we stood toward it, and several hours passed before we discovered that it was a separate island—the island of Roti, as we afterward learned.

Shortly after Mr. Bligh had altered our course to return to the coast we had left, I lost all knowledge of what went on. The sun had been extremely hot, and we had no protection from its rays. It may be that I suffered a slight stroke, and this, combined with my other miseries, had proven too much for me. At any rate, I sank into a stupor which left me a dim consciousness of misery and of little else. Now and then I heard the confused murmur of voices, and I vaguely remember having been roused from frightful dreams, when I thought I was struggling alone in the sea and upon the point of drowning, to find that I was still in the launch, being raised up to escape the water that came over the side. I was, indeed, far gone, powerless to do aught for myself. Then followed a period of complete darkness, when I was nothing but an inert mass of skin and bones; and my next recollection was of someone repeatedly calling my name. Try as I would, I could not rouse myself sufficiently to reply. I heard Bligh's voice: "Give him the whole of it, Mr. Nelson. He'll come round."

And so I did. A quarter of a pint of rum was poured down my gullet. I remember how the heat and the strength of it seemed to flow into every part of me, clearing my brain and giving me a blessed sense of well-being; but oh! more blessed was the sound of Nelson's voice: "Ledward! Ledward! We're here, old fellow!"

It was deep night, the cloudless sky sprinkled with stars dimmed by the soft splendour of the waning moon. I found myself sitting propped up in the stern sheets. Nelson was kneeling beside me, and Cole supporting me with his arm around my shoulders. As I turned my head, Cole said: "That's what was needed, sir; he's coming round nicely."

I was conscious of a feeling of shame and vexation that I, the *Bounty's* surgeon, should be in such a deplorable state — an encumbrance instead of a help to the others.

"What's this, Nelson?" I faltered. "Damme! Have I been asleep?"

"Don't talk, Ledward," he replied. "Look! Look yonder! . . . Turn him a little, Mr. Cole."

The boatswain lifted me gently so that I sat half facing forward. The sail had been lowered, and there were six men at the oars, pulling slowly and feebly across what appeared to be the head of a great bay, so calm that the wavering reflection of the moon lay on the surface of the water. Outlines of the land were clearly revealed; not half a mile away I could see two square-rigged vessels lying at anchor, and beyond them, on a high foreshore, what appeared to be a fort whose walls gleamed faintly in the mild light.

"Easy, lads," Bligh called to the men at the oars, "don't exert yourselves"; and then, to me: "How is it with you, Mr. Ledward? I was bound you shouldn't miss this moment."

I could not speak. I hesitate to admit it, but I could not. I was weak as a six-months' child, and now, for the first time, tears gushed from my eyes. They were not tears of relief, of joy at our deliverance. No. I could have controlled those. But when I looked at Mr. Bligh, sitting at his old position with his hand on the tiller, there welled up within me a feeling toward him that destroyed the barriers we Englishmen are so proud of erecting against one another. I saw him then as he deserved to be seen, in a light that transfigured him. Enough. The deepest emotions of the heart are not lightly to be spoken of, and no words of mine could add to the stature of the captain of the *Bounty's* launch.

I managed at length to say: "I'm doing very well, sir," and left it at that.

The silence of the land seemed to flow down upon us, healing our weary hearts, filling us with a deep content that made all speech superfluous. The launch moved forward as smoothly as though she were gliding through air, and the faint creak of the oars against the tholepins and the gentle plash of the blades in the water were sounds by which to measure the vastness of this peace.

It was then about three in the morning. Nearer we came and nearer to the little town hushed in sleep; not even a dog was astir to bay at the moon. As we drew in we saw that the two ships were anchored a considerable distance to the right of the fort and about a cable-length from shore. We made out a small cutter riding near them, and not a light showing in any of these vessels.

We turned then to approach an open space on the beach that appeared to be a point of embarkation for boats, and Mr. Cole made his way to the bow. A fishing line with a stone attached served as our lead line. At Mr. Bligh's order, Tinkler began heaving it. "Six fathoms, sir," he called. We moved slowly on into shallower water. In the moonlight we could now see the ghostly gleam of roofs and walls, embowered in trees and flowering shrubs whose perfume floated out to us with the cool, moist air that flowed down from the valley of the interior.

"Way enough!" said Bligh, and then: "Drop the grapnel, Mr. Cole."

The oars were gotten in; there was a light splash as the grapnel went over the side. The boatswain paid out the line and made fast. Our voyage was at an end.

There were but eight of our company strong enough to sit upon the thwarts; the others were lying or sitting, propped up in the bottom of the boat.

"Let us pray, lads," said Bligh. We bowed our heads while he returned thanks to Almighty God.

We lay within thirty or forty yards of the beach. A little distance to the right, the walls of the fort rose from their ramparts of rock. All was silent there; not so much as a gleam of light appeared anywhere in the settlement. Captain Bligh hailed the fort repeatedly, with no result.

"Try your voice on 'em, Mr. Purcell," he said.

Purcell hailed, then the boatswain, then the two together; but there was no response.

"By God," said Bligh, "were we at war with the Dutch, I'll warrant we could capture the place, weak as we are, with nothing but four rusty cutlasses. They've not so much as a sentinel on the walls."

"We've roused someone at last," said Nelson. "Look yonder."

A strange-looking man was just emerging from the shadows of the trees lining the road that led to the beach. He was clad only in shirt and trousers, and had what appeared to be a white nightcap on his head. He was exceedingly fat, and walked at a waddling gait.

"Can you speak English, my good man?" Bligh called.

He came forward another pace or two, as though for a clearer view of us, but made no reply.

"I say, can you speak English? You understand?"

Whether it were astonishment, or fear, or both, or neither, that moved him, we were at a loss to know; but of a sudden he turned on his incredibly short legs and waddled away at twice the speed with which he had approached.

"Ahoy there!" Bligh called after him. "Don't go! Wait, I say!"

The man turned, shouted something in a deep, powerful voice, and disappeared under the shadow of the trees.

"Was it Dutch he spoke, Nelson?" Bligh asked.

"Undoubtedly," said Nelson; "but that is as much as I can say. . . . We shall fare well here, that's plain."

Bligh laughed. "Aye, so we shall, if that fellow is an average specimen of the inhabitants. Damn his eyes! What possessed him to run off like that?"

"Likely he's gone for help, sir. There may be English-speaking people here."

"Let us hope so, Mr. Fryer. Possess your souls in patience, lads. We must not go ashore without permission, and that we shall soon have, I promise you. Dawn is scarcely an hour off."

In a little time the Dutchman returned with another man dressed in a seaman's uniform.

"Ahoy, there! What boat is that?" called the latter.

"Who are you?" Bligh replied. "An Englishman?"

"Aye, sir."

"Is there an English ship here?"

"No, sir."

"Then how came you in these parts, my man?" said Bligh, with something of his old quarter-deck manner.

"I'm quartermaster's mate, sir, of the Dutch vessel yonder. Captain Spikerman."

"Good!" said Bligh. "Listen carefully, young man! Tell your captain — what's his name, again?"

"Spikerman, sir."

"Tell Captain Spikerman that Captain Bligh, of His Majesty's armed transport *Bounty,* wishes to see him at his very earliest convenience. Inform him that the matter is pressing. You understand?"

"Aye, aye, sir."

"Very well; carry him this message instantly. Don't fear to rouse him. He will thank you for doing so."

"Aye, aye, sir. He's sleeping ashore. I'll go this instant."

We must have waited a full three quarters of an hour, although the time seemed immeasurably longer. The delay, as we were to learn, was not Captain

Spikerman's fault. He resided in a distant part of the town, and came as soon as he could dress.

Dawn was at hand, and the people in the town were stirring out of their houses, when we saw him approaching with two of his officers and the man who had carried our message. Captain Bligh stood up in the stern sheets. His clothing was a mass of rags revealing his frightfully emaciated limbs; his haggard, bony face was covered with a month's growth of beard; but he held himself as erect as though he were standing on the *Bounty's* quarter-deck.

"Captain Spikerman?" he called.

For a few seconds the little group on shore stared at us in silence. Captain Spikerman stepped forward. "At your service, sir," he replied.

"Captain Bligh, of His Majesty's armed transport *Bounty*. We are in need of assistance, sir. I will be grateful indeed if you will secure us permission to land."

"You may come ashore at once, Captain Bligh. I can vouch for the governor's permission. Your boat may be brought directly to the beach."

"Haul in the grapnel, Mr. Cole. Two men at the oars." Tinkler and Hayward hauled it in, Cole coiling the line neatly as they did so. Peckover and Purcell took the oars, and the launch proceeded on the last fifty yards of a voyage of more than three thousand, six hundred miles. "Easy, Mr. Cole! Don't let her touch!"

The boatswain fended off with our bamboo pole and attempted to leap out to hold her, but the poor fellow had forgotten his condition. His legs gave way and he fell into the water, holding on to the gunwale, until, with a grim effort, he managed to get his footing. Tinkler threw a line ashore which the English seaman of the Dutch ship took up. Captain Spikerman and his officers stood for a moment as though powerless to move. Then, taking in our situation, they themselves sprang into the shallow water to draw us alongside.

"God in heaven, Captain Bligh! What is this? From what place do you come?" Mr. Spikerman exclaimed.

"That you shall know in good time, sir," said Bligh; "but I must first see to my men. Some of them are in a pitiable state from starvation. Is there a place in the town where they may be cared for?"

"You may take them directly to my house. One moment, sir."

Captain Spikerman turned to one of his officers and spoke to him rapidly in the Dutch tongue. The young man made off at once, half running along the road to the town.

By this time a crowd of the townspeople had collected about us, and others came from moment to moment. They were of various nationalities,— Dutch, Malays, Chinese, and people evidently of mixed blood,— and they stared at us with expressions of mingled horror and pity. Meanwhile, those of us who could had gotten out of the launch; but more than half of the company had to be carried ashore. We were taken a little way up the beach, where mats were spread for us on the sand. There we waited the arrival of conveyances which were to carry us to Captain Spikerman's house, while the townspeople gathered in a wide circle, gazing at us as though they would never have done.

Of our people, Lebogue was in the most serious condition. The old fellow lay close beside me. He was no more than a skeleton covered with skin; but his was a resolute spirit, and, weak as he was, he yet had within him a strong will to live. Nelson, Simpson, Hall, Smith, and myself were in a plight only a little less grave. Nelson tried to walk ashore, but after a few steps his legs gave way and he was constrained to allow himself to be carried. Hallet was very weak, but managed to keep his footing. Poor Elphinstone's disabilities were, as I have said, mental rather than physical. His face still wore its vacant, puzzled expression, and he appeared to have no knowledge of his surroundings.

In a short while, Mr. Spikerman's lieutenant returned with litters and a score of Malay chair-men. They carried us into the town, Mr. Bligh and the stronger of the company following on foot. I have only a dim recollection of the way we went, past shops and warehouses, and along shaded streets, till we came to a pleasant house in an elevated situation where Captain Spikerman lived. He and his officers were kindness itself; I shall ever have a feeling of sincere liking for the people of the Dutch nation because of the humane treatment we received from those members of it who resided at Coupang. Such was the name of the haven — which I might better call "heaven" — at which we had arrived.

When we had been bathed with warm water our sores were dressed by Mr. Max, the surgeon of the town; whereupon we were placed in beds and given a little hot soup, or tea, which was all that our stomachs could receive at this time. I am speaking here of the greatest invalids amongst us, who were cared for in one room. Captain Bligh, when he had bathed and refreshed himself with food and a few hours' sleep, accompanied Captain Spikerman to the house of Mr. Timotheus Wanjon, the secretary to Mr. Van Este, the governor of the town. Mr. Van Este was at this time lying very ill, and incapable of transacting any business.

On this day I had the sweetest sleep I have ever enjoyed in my life. The cooling ointment with which my sores had been dressed, and the soft bed upon which I lay, lulled me to rest within half an hour. I was aroused, toward evening, to take a little soup and bread, but fell to sleep again immediately after, and did not waken until about ten of the clock the following morning.

After four days of complete rest, we were wonderfully restored, and all except Lebogue could rise from bed and walk a little in Mr. Spikerman's garden. His services to us were endless; he had put us under obligations we shall never be able to repay, but we did not, of course, wish to discommode him longer than was absolutely necessary. All his rooms were taken up by our company, and he was sleeping at the house of Mr. Wanjon. Captain Bligh found that there was but one available house in the settlement. Having examined it, he decided that we should all lodge there. Mr. Spikerman suggested that the house be taken by Captain Bligh for himself and his officers, and that the men be accommodated on one of the vessels lying in the harbour, but Captain Bligh was not willing at such a time to fare better than his men. Therefore, on our fifth day in Coupang, we removed to our new quarters.

The dwelling contained a hall with a room at each end, and was surrounded with a piazza. Above, there was a spacious, airy loft. One room was reserved to Captain Bligh; Nelson, Fryer, Peckover, and myself lodged in the other, and the men were assigned to the loft. The hall was common to all of the officers, and the back piazza was set aside for the use of the people. In order to simplify the matter of our victualing, the three midshipmen readily agreed to mess with the men. Through the kindness of Mr. Van Este, the house was furnished with beds, tables, chairs, settees — everything, in fact, of which we stood in need; and our food was dressed at his own house and brought to us by his servants.

Mr. Van Este expressed a desire to see Captain Bligh and some of his officers. It was therefore arranged that Mr. Bligh, Nelson, and myself should wait upon him, in company with Mr. Wanjon and Captain Spikerman. We found the governor propped up in bed, so wasted by his illness that he looked — as, indeed, he was — at death's door. His voice was exceedingly weak, but his eyes were full of interest. Captain Spikerman acted as our interpreter. He acquainted the governor with the circumstances of the mutiny. Mr. Van Este was not aware of the position of Tofoa and the Friendly Islands; in fact, I believe that he did not know of their existence. When he had been told that we had made a voyage in the ship's launch of above three thousand, six hundred miles, he raised a thin white hand and said but one word in reply. Captain Spikerman turned to Mr. Bligh.

"Mr. Van Este says 'Impossible,' Captain Bligh. You will understand that this is only a manner of speaking, to convey his astonishment. He does not doubt your word."

Bligh smiled faintly. "You may tell Mr. Van Este that he is right: it *was* impossible; nevertheless, we did it."

He then conveyed, through Mr. Spikerman, our

gratitude for the kind and hospitable treatment we had received, and we took our leave. The governor was far too ill to bear the fatigue of a long conversation.

This day, June the nineteenth, was remarkable for still another reason. Mr. Max, my Dutch colleague, and I had agreed that our company need not be kept longer on a diet. Mr. Wanjon, who himself overlooked the matter of our victualing, had provided a feast equal to the greatness of the occasion; and he, Captain Spikerman, and Mr. Max readily consented to join us at table. On our way from the governor's house, we called for Mr. Max, and then proceeded to our residence, where the men were already at their dinner on the back piazza. Cole sat at the head of the table, with the midshipmen on either side and the others below. Even Lebogue had sufficiently recovered to be present. The table was loaded with food that would have gladdened any seaman's eyes; it was a pleasure to see the half-starved men stowing it away.

At Captain Bligh's entrance, they rose; but he at once motioned them to be seated.

"Eat hearty, lads," he said. "There's no need to wish you good appetites, that's plain."

"We're doin' famous, sir," Cole replied. A moment later, Captain Bligh retired with our guests to the hall, while Nelson and I remained for a little to look on at this memorable feast.

"I hope you'll not think we're goin' beyond reason, Mr. Ledward," said Cole. "Better vittles I never tasted!"

"And well you deserve them, every man of you," I replied. "Eat as much as you like."

"Aye, they'll do," said Purcell, grudgingly; "but I'd sooner set down to a good feed of eggs and bacon. All these rich faldelals . . . I don't well know what I'm eatin'."

"Trust old Chips to find fault," said Hayward.

"Here, Purcell; have some of the bread, if you don't like Dutch food," said Hallet. "Pass it along to him, Tinkler."

"Mr. Nelson and Mr. Ledward would like some, I'm sure," said Tinkler. "Try a little, Mr. Nelson."

He rose and took up a large platter, set high in the middle of the table on four tall water-glasses. Heaped on the platter was something that resembled nothing on earth save what it was: the bread of the *Bounty's* launch.

"Well, I'm damned!" said Nelson, with a laugh.

"Have just a crumb as an appetizer. We did, the lot of us," said Tinkler. "Mr. Ledward, what about you?"

"Wait!" Hayward exclaimed. "Don't you give 'em a ration, Tinkler, without weighing it. Where's Captain Bligh's scales?"

It warmed my heart to see them in such a merry mood, and the *Bounty* bread — the sight of it, at least

—was indeed the best of reminders of misery past and done with.

"Is this all that was left in the launch, Tinkler?" Nelson asked.

"Yes, sir."

"We've been making an estimate, Mr. Nelson," said Hayward. "What you see on the platter would have lasted the eighteen of us another eleven days, had we not had the abominable misfortune of finding Coupang."

"Save for our abominable luck in landing amongst the Dutch, we might even have got home on it," Tinkler added. "What do you think, boatswain?"

Cole looked up from his plate, holding his fork erect in his fist.

"I'll say this, Mr. Tinkler," he replied gravely. "If Captain Bligh was forced to take us all the way to England in the launch, with no more bread than what's on that plate, I'll warrant he could do it if we'd back him up."

At Cole's words there was a cheer, in which every man at the table joined heartily.

"But don't, for God's sake, suggest it, boatswain!" said Hayward in a low voice. "He might want to try."

The dinner at the captain's table proceeded more soberly. There was food, food, and more food: curried prawns with rice, baked fish with rice, roast fowl with rice, and many other dishes, with excellent wine and schnapps to wash all down. We of the *Bounty's* launch had been so long accustomed to thinking of wine and spirits as the most precious of commodities, to be taken only a spoonful at a time, that it was hard to convince ourselves that we need no longer be sparing of them. Captain Bligh, always a moderate drinker, was still sparing; but the rest of us did better justice to the good cheer; and our Dutch companions ate and drank with as much zest as though they had been members of our company all the way from Tofoa. Nelson threw a quizzical glance in my direction, toward the end of the meal, when they were attacking new dishes with undiminished appetite.

Our guests were naturally curious about the events of the mutiny, but they soon realized that it was a sore subject with Mr. Bligh, which he preferred not to discuss.

"You have our sworn affidavits, Mr. Wanjon," he remarked, at this time. "The facts are there, attested to by every one of my men. It is not likely that the villains will come this way, but should they do so, seize and hold them. Let not one of them escape."

"You may set your mind at rest on that score," Mr. Wanjon replied; and with this the discussion of the mutiny was dropped.

"I greatly desire to proceed homeward as soon as my men are fit to travel," Bligh remarked. He laughed in a wry manner. "We are a company of paupers, Mr. Wanjon. We've not a shilling amongst us; not a halfpenny bit!"

"Do not let that worry you, Captain Bligh. Mr. Van Este has instructed me to provide you with whatever funds you may desire."

"That's uncommon kind of him. I shall draw bills on His Majesty's Government. . . . Captain Spikerman, is there a small vessel to be had hereabout —one fit to carry us to Batavia? I wish to arrive there in time to sail home with your October fleet."

"There is a small schooner lying in a cove about two leagues distant," Captain Spikerman replied. "She can be bought, I know, for one thousand rix-dollars."

"Pretty dear, isn't it?" said Bligh.

"She's well worth it, I assure you. She is thirty-four feet long, perfectly sound, and would serve your purpose admirably. Should you care to look at her, I can have her here for your inspection within a day or two."

"Excellent," said Bligh. "I'll be greatly obliged to you."

The dinner was at an end, and presently our guests left us. Nelson was in a jubilant mood. He had asked permission to botanize the island in the environs of Coupang, and Mr. Wanjon not only agreed but had offered to provide servants to accompany him on his expeditions. Nelson was in no fit state to go abroad, and I demurred strongly against the plan. However, he had won Captain Bligh's consent and would listen to none of my objections. As a matter of fact, I would gladly have gone with him, had it not been that my ulcered leg made walking out of the question.

During the next ten days he was constantly away from Coupang, returning only occasionally to bring in his specimens. At first he appeared to thrive upon the work, but I soon realized that he was exerting himself far beyond his strength. Early in July he came down with an inflammatory fever which at last confined him to his bed, whether he would or no. Mr. Max and I both attended him, but his condition grew steadily worse. His weakened constitution had been tried too severely, and it was soon plain to both of us that he was dying.

He passed away on the twentieth of July, at one o'clock of the morning. I need not say how his loss affected our company. He was respected and loved by every one of us. In my own case, we had been friends from the day of our first meeting at Spithead, and I had looked forward to many years of his friendship. As for Mr. Bligh, Nelson was, I believe, one of three or four men whom he held in his heart of hearts. I think he would sooner have lost the half of his company than to have lost him.

We buried him the following day. His coffin was carried by twelve soldiers from the fort, dressed in

black. Mr. Bligh and Mr. Wanjon walked immediately behind the bier; then came ten gentlemen of
the town and the officers from the ships in the harbour; and the *Bounty's* people followed after. Mr.
Bligh read the service, and it was as much as he could
do to go through with it. The body was laid to
rest behind the chapel, in that part of the cemetery
set aside for Europeans.

I recall with little pleasure the remainder of our
sojourn in Coupang. Mr. Bligh was constantly employed about the business of our departure, and the
Bounty's people were daily aboard the schooner he had
bought, making her ready for sea. In my own case,
I was as useless now as I had been much of the time
in the *Bounty's* launch. My ulcer would not heal,
and I was forced to sit in idleness on the piazza of our
dwelling, thinking of Nelson, and how gladly he
would have lived to go home with us.

The schooner was a staunch little craft, as Captain
Spikerman had assured us. Bligh named her *Resource*, and, as we were to go along the Java coast,
which is infested with small, piratical vessels, he armed
her with four brass swivels and fourteen stand of
small arms, with an abundance of powder and shot.

On the twentieth of August, being entirely prepared for sea, we spent the morning in waiting upon
our various Dutch friends, whose kindness had been
unremitting from the day of our arrival at Coupang.
Mr. Van Este, the governor, was lying at the very

point of death, and Captain Bligh was not able to see
him. Mr. Wanjon received us in his stead, and Mr.
Bligh tendered him our grateful thanks for the innumerable services he had rendered us. Mr. Max,
the surgeon, who had cared for our people when I
was unable to do so, would accept no remuneration
for his attendance upon us, saying that he had done
no more than his duty. His action was typical of
that of others at Coupang who had been our hosts
for more than two months.

Throughout the afternoon our hosts became our
guests on board the *Resource,* and we showed them
what small hospitalities our poor means afforded.

Captain Bligh looked his old self again. He was
now cloathed as befitted his rank, and his hair was
neatly dressed and powdered. As he stood on the
after-deck, talking with Captain Spikerman and Mr.
Wanjon, I could not but remark the contrast between
his appearance now and what it had been upon our
arrival at Coupang. Nevertheless, as I observed him,
I was conscious of a curious feeling of disappointment. It may be thought strange, but I liked him
better as he was in the *Bounty's* launch: rags hanging
from his wasted limbs, his hand on the tiller, the
great seas foaming up behind him, and the low scud
flying close overhead. There he was unique, one man
in ten thousand. On the after-deck of the *Resource,*
he appeared to be merely one of the innumerable
captains of His Majesty's Navy. But well I knew in

my heart the quality of the man who stood there. Forty-one days in a ship's boat had taught me that.

Toward four of the afternoon, the last of our guests returned to the shore. The breeze favouring, we weighed at once and stood off toward the open sea. The beach was thronged with people waving hats and handkerchiefs, and as we drew away the air quivered with the parting salute from the fort. Mr. Peck-over, our gunner, was rejoiced to be employed for the first time this long while in his proper duties. Our brass swivels replied bravely to the Dutch salu-tation.

As for the *Bounty's* launch, she was towing be-hind, with Tinkler at the tiller, proud of the honour conferred upon him. Peckover and I were standing at the rail, looking down upon her in silence, think-ing of her faithful service. We loved her, every man of us, as though she were a sentient being.

Presently Peckover turned to me. "How well she tows," he said. "She seems to want to come. Though we had no line to her, I'll warrant she'd still follow Captain Bligh."

"By God, Peckover," I said, "I believe she would!"

Epilogue

On the first of October we cast anchor in Batavia Road, near a Dutch man-of-war. More than a score of East Indiamen were riding there, as well as a great fleet of native prows. The captain went ashore at once, to call on Mr. Englehard, the Sabandar — an officer with whom all strangers are obliged to transact their business; and on the same evening we were informed that we might lodge at an hotel, the only place in the city where foreigners are permitted to reside.

The climate of Batavia is one of the most unwholesome in the world. The miasmatic effluvia which rise from the river during the night bring on an intermittent fever, or paludism, often of great severity, accompanied by unendurable headaches. Weakened by our privations, some of us fell immediate victims to this disorder, which was to cost Lenkletter and Elphinstone their lives. The hotel, where I resided with the other officers, though situated in what is considered a healthy quarter of the city, and near the river bank, was intolerably hot, and so ill arranged for a free circulation of air that a man in robust health must soon have succumbed to its stifling rooms.

After one night in this place, Mr. Bligh was taken

with a fever so violent that I feared for his life. I
was unable to attend him, since I was suffering from
a fever as well as from the ulcer on my leg, and Mr.
Aansorp, head surgeon of the town hospital, was sent
for. By administering bark of Peru and wine, this
skillful physician so improved Captain Bligh that
within a day he was able once more to transact the
pressing business on his hands.

We had been four days at the hotel when Mr.
Sparling, Surgeon-General of Java, had the kindness
to invite Captain Bligh and me to be his guests at
the seamen's hospital, on an island in the river, three
or four miles from the town. This hospital is a
model of its kind, large enough to accommodate fifteen hundred men. The sick receive excellent care
and attention, and the wards are scrupulously clean.
Mr. Sparling, who had been educated in England,
listened with great interest to the account of our
voyage, and insisted that Captain Bligh send for those
of his people who were ill. Late one afternoon I
was sitting on my colleague's shady verandah. He
was smoking a long black *cigarro;* I lay on a settee
with my bandaged leg stretched out on a stool. We
were discussing the medical phases of our sufferings,
Mr. Sparling expressing surprise that any man in the
launch should have survived.

"You say that three of the people were forty-one
days without evacuation?" he asked. "It is all but
incredible!"

"So much so," I replied, "that I hope to write a paper to be read before the College of Surgeons. What little we ate appeared to be entirely used up by our bodies."

"It is a miracle that you are alive. But your constitutions have been too much impaired to withstand such a climate as this. I am concerned about Mr. Bligh. Should he stay long . . ." He shrugged his shoulders, paused for a moment, and went on: "I have never known a man of greater determination! With such a fever, most men would be on their backs. Yet he goes daily into the town to transact his business. I have spoken to the governor. Mr. Bligh will be permitted to take passage, with two others, on the packet sailing on the sixteenth of this month."

"You are kind indeed, sir! Mr. Bligh shared all of our sufferings, and, in addition, the entire responsibility was his. The strain had impaired his health gravely; I have feared more than once that he might leave his bones here."

"That possibility is by no means remote," said Sparling. "There is a high mortality here amongst Europeans. Mr. Bligh, I can see, is a man who will attend to his duty even to the serious prejudice of his health. Do what you can, Mr. Ledward, to urge upon him the necessity for caution."

"I have, sir," I replied; "you may be sure of that; but he cannot, or will not, take advice."

My colleague nodded. "He's a strong-headed man, that's plain. I should imagine that he was a bit of a tartar on the quarter-deck?"

At that moment a Malay servant appeared in the doorway, bowed, and spoke to his master. Mr. Sparling rose.

"Captain Bligh is disembarking now," he said, as he left me.

Presently he ushered Bligh to a chair and made a sign to the servant, who brought in a tray with glasses, and a decanter of excellent Cape Town wine.

"Let me prescribe a glass of wine," remarked Sparling. "There is no finer tonic for men in your condition."

"Your health, sir," said Bligh, "and that of our kind hostess, if I may propose it. I have had a hard day in the town; your house is a haven of refuge for a weary man."

His face was gaunt and flushed, and his eyes unnaturally bright, as he sat in one of Sparling's long rattan chairs, wearing an ill-fitting suit of cloathes, made by a Chinese tailor in the town.

"One of your men is very low," remarked the Surgeon-General presently; "the one we visited this morning. I fear there is little hope for him."

"Aye — Hall," said Bligh. "Poor fellow."

"The flux seems deadly in these parts," I observed.

"Yes," said Sparling. "Few recover from the

violent form of the disease. He must have eaten of some infected fruits in Coupang."

We were silent for a time, while Bligh seemed to be brooding over some unpleasant thought.

"Ledward, I've had to part with the launch!" he exclaimed at last.

"You've sold her, sir?" I asked.

"Yes. And the schooner, too — but she meant little to me. As for the launch, though I am a poor man, I would gladly give five hundred pounds to take her home!"

"You could get no space for her on the *Vlydte?*"

"Not a foot! Damme! Not an inch! Not even for my six pots of plants from Timor."

Sparling nodded. "There are never enough ships in the October fleet," he remarked. "Every foot of space and every passage has been bespoken for months. It was only through the governor's influence that I got passage for you and your two men. Should my wife desire to send a few gifts of native manufacture to her uncle at the Cape of Good Hope, I declare to you it would be impossible at this time!"

"I had hoped to take the launch," said Bligh. "She should be placed in the museum of the Admiralty. A finer boat was never built! I love her, every frame and plank!"

"How did you fare at the auction?" asked Sparling.

Bligh laughed ruefully. "Damned badly!" he replied. "If I may remark upon it, sir, your method of conducting an auction strikes me as inferior to ours."

"Yes, from the seller's standpoint. I have attended your English auctions. Where the bids mount higher and higher, the bidders are apt to lose their heads."

"You should have been there, Ledward," said Bligh. "They set a high figure at first, which the auctioneer brings down gradually until someone bids. Small danger of losing one's head when there can be only one bid! Several Dutch captains were on hand; half a dozen Malays, a Chinaman or two, and some others—God knows what they may have been! There was one Englishman present besides ourselves, —Captain John Eddie, commanding a ship from Bengal. He'd come merely to look on, not to bid. The auctioneer put up the schooner first, at two thousand rix-dollars. The figure came down to three hundred, without an offer! By God, Mr. Sparling, a Scot or a Jew would starve to death in competition with your seafaring countrymen! At three hundred, an old Chinaman showed signs of interest, casting shrewd glances at a Dutch captain standing close by. At two hunderd and ninety-five, Captain Eddie raised his hand. By God! I was grateful to him for that! The price was not a third of her value, but Eddie kept those bloody sharks from getting her. It warmed my heart to see their disappointment."

"What did the launch fetch?" I asked.

"Let us not speak of her. Cole and Peckover were

with me; they felt as badly as I. If I could have left her here, in safe hands, until there was a chance to send her home . . ." He sighed. "It couldn't be arranged. It cost me dear to see her go!"

On the following day died Thomas Hall, our third loss since leaving the *Bounty*. He had endured manfully our hardships in the launch, only to succumb to the most dreaded of East Indian diseases. Lenkletter and Elphinstone, destined also to leave their bones in Batavia, were suffering with the same paludism that had attacked Captain Bligh.

At this time the Sabandar informed us that every officer and man must make deposition before a notary concerning the mutiny on board the *Bounty*, in order to authorize the government to detain her, should she venture into Dutch waters. Bligh considered this unlikely; but his determination to see the mutineers brought to justice was such that he left no contingency unprovided for.

On the morning of October sixteenth I was awakened long before daylight by sounds in Mr. Bligh's room, next to mine. He was to be rowed down the river to go on board the *Vlydte*, and I could hear him, through the thin wall, directing his servant, Smith, how to pack the large camphorwood box he had purchased some days before.

In the gray light of dawn, Mr. Bligh knocked at my door and entered the room.

"Awake, Ledward?" he asked.   I struggled to sit up, but he motioned me not to move.

"I've come to bid you good-bye," he said.

"I wish I were sailing with you, sir!"

He laughed his short, harsh laugh. "Damme! I'm by no means sure you're not the luckier of the two!   You may have the good fortune to go home on an English ship.   Yesterday I called on Captain Couvret, aboard the *Vlydte;* we had some talk concerning the manner of navigation.   They carry no log, and scarcely steer within a quarter of a point. No wonder they frequently find themselves above ten degrees out in their reckoning!   The state of discipline on board is appalling to an English seaman. It will be a miracle if we reach Table Bay; once there, I hope to transfer to an English ship."

"Permit me to wish you a good voyage, in any case."

At that moment Mr. Sparling called from the piazza: "Your boat is waiting, Captain Bligh!"

Bligh took my hand in a brief, warm clasp.

"Good-bye, Ledward," he said. "Don't fail to call on Mrs. Bligh when you reach London."

"I shall hope to see you, too, sir."

He shook his head. "It's not likely.   If I have my way, I shall sail for Otaheite before you reach England."

He was gone — the finest seaman under whom I have ever had the good fortune to sail. From the bottom of my heart I wished him God Speed.

THE RUN OF THE LAUNCH

(From the Island of Tofoa to Coupang, on the Island of Timor)

Year 1789		No. of Miles
May	3	86
	4	95
	5	94
	6	84
	7	79
	8	62
	9	64
	10	78
	11	102
	12	89
	13	79
	14	89
	15	(no record)
	16	101
	17	100
	18	106
	19	100
	20	75
	21	99
	22	130
	23	116
	24	114
	25	108
	26	112
	27	109
	28	(no record) Entered the Great Barrier Reef

29	. . . . . .	18	To Restoration Island
30	. . . . . .	—	At Restoration Island
31	. . . . . .	30	To Sunday Island
June 1	. . . . . .	10	To Lagoon Island
2	. . . . . .	30	
3	. . . . . .	35	To Turtle Island
4	. . . . . .	111	Clear of New Holland
5	. . . . . .	108	
6	. . . . . .	117	
7	. . . . . .	88	
8	. . . . . .	106	
9	. . . . . .	107	
10	. . . . . .	111	
11	. . . . . .	109	
12	. . . . . .	(no record)	Sighted Timor
13	. . . . . .	54	Coasting Timor
14	. . . . . .	(no record)	Reached Coupang

Total distance run, 3618 miles

THE TRILOGY OF THE "BOUNTY"

CHARLES NORDHOFF and James Norman Hall began in 1929
their preliminary work upon an historical novel dealing with
the mutiny on board H.M.S. *Bounty*. It was at first antici-
pated that one or both of the authors would have to journey
to England and elsewhere to collect the necessary source material, but, upon the advice of their publishers, this research
was delegated to competent English assistants. With their
painstaking help, the archives of the British Museum were
searched through, as well as the rare-book shops and the col-
lections of prints and engravings in London, for all procur-
able material dealing not only with the history of the *Bounty*,
but also with life and discipline in the British Navy during
the late eighteenth and early nineteenth centuries. With the
generous permission of the British Admiralty, photostat copies
were made of Bligh's correspondence and of the Admiralty
records of the court-martial proceedings. Copies of the
Bounty's deck and rigging plans were also secured, with
special reference to the alterations made for her breadfruit-
tree voyage; and a British naval officer, whose interest in these
matters had been aroused, then proceeded to build an exact
model of the vessel.

Books, engravings, blueprints, photostats, and photographs
were finally assembled and sent to the publishers' office, where
the shipment was checked, supplemented with material collected from American sources, and forwarded to its final
destination, Tahiti, the home of Nordhoff and Hall.

THE TRILOGY OF THE "BOUNTY"

The *Bounty* history divides itself naturally into three parts, and it was the plan of the authors, from the beginning, to deal with each of these in a separate volume, in case sufficient public interest was shown in the first to justify the preparation of the trilogy.

Mutiny on the Bounty, which opens the story, is concerned with the voyage of the vessel from England, the long Tahiti sojourn while the cargo of young breadfruit trees was being assembled, the departure of the homeward-bound ship, the mutiny, and the fate of those of her company who later returned to Tahiti, where they were eventually seized by H.M.S. *Pandora* and taken back to England for trial.

The authors chose as the narrator of this story a fictitious character, Roger Byam, who tells it as an old man, after his retirement from the Navy. Byam had his actual counterpart in the person of Peter Heywood, whose name was, for this reason, omitted from the roster of the *Bounty's* company. Midshipman Byam's experience follows closely that of Midshipman Heywood. With the license of historical novelists, the authors based the career of Byam upon that of Heywood, but in depicting it they did not, of course, follow the latter in every detail. In the essentials relating to the mutiny and its aftermath, they have adhered to the facts long preserved in the records of the British Admiralty.

Men against the Sea, the second narrative, is the story of Captain Bligh and the eighteen loyal men who, on the morning of the mutiny, were set adrift by the mutineers in the *Bounty's* launch, an open boat but twenty-three feet long, in which they made a 3600-mile voyage from the scene of the mutiny to Timor, in the Dutch East Indies. Captain Bligh's log of this remarkable voyage, a series of brief daily notes, was, of course, the chief literary source of this second novel. The voyage is described in the words of one of those who survived it — Thomas Ledward, acting surgeon of the *Bounty,* whose medical knowledge and whose experience in reading men's sufferings would qualify him as a sensitive and reliable observer.

Pitcairn's Island, the concluding story, is, perhaps, the strangest and most romantic. After two unsuccessful attempts to settle on the island of Tupuai (or Tubuai, as it is more commonly spelled in these days), the mutineers returned to Tahiti, where they parted company. Fletcher Christian, acting lieutenant of the *Bounty* and instigator of the mutiny, once more embarked in the ship for an unknown destination. With him were eight of his own men and eighteen Polynesians (twelve women and six men). They sailed from Tahiti in September 1789, and for a period of eighteen years nothing more was heard of them. In February 1808, the American sealing vessel *Topaz*, calling at Pitcairn, discovered on this supposedly uninhabited crumb of land a thriving community of mixed blood: a number of middle-aged Polynesian women and more than a score of children, ruled by a white-haired English seaman, Alexander Smith, the only survivor of the fifteen men who had landed there so long before.

The story of what befell the refugees during the eighteen years before the arrival of the *Topaz* offers a fitting conclusion to the tale of the *Bounty* mutiny. As the authors have said, in their Note to *Pitcairn's Island*, the only source of information we now have concerning the events of those years is the account — or, more accurately, the several discrepant accounts — handed on to us by the sea captains who visited Pitcairn during Smith's latter years. It is upon these accounts that their story is based.

Those who are interested in the source material concerning the *Bounty* mutiny will find an exhaustive bibliography of books, articles, and unpublished manuscripts in the Appendix to Mr. George Mackaness's splendid *Life of Vice-Admiral William Bligh*, published by Messrs. Angus and Robertson, of Sydney, Australia. Among the sources consulted by

THE TRILOGY OF THE "BOUNTY"

Nordhoff and Hall were the following: "Minutes of the Proceedings of a Court-Martial on Lieutenant William Bligh and certain members of his crew, to investigate the cause of the loss of H.M.S. *Bounty*"; *A Narrative of the Mutiny on Board His Majesty's Ship "Bounty,"* by William Bligh; *A Voyage to the South Sea,* by William Bligh; *The Life of Vice-Admiral William Bligh,* by George Mackaness; *Mutineers of the "Bounty" and Their Descendants in Pitcairn and Norfolk Islands,* by Lady Belcher; *The Mutiny and Piratical Seizure of H.M.S. "Bounty,"* by Sir John Barrow; *Bligh of the "Bounty,"* by Geoffrey Rawson; *Voyage of H.M.S. "Pandora,"* by E. Edwards and G. Hamilton; Cook's *Voyages;* Hawkesworth's *Voyages;* Beechey's *Voyages;* Bougainville's *Voyages;* Ellis's *Polynesian Researches;* *Pitcairn Island and the Islanders,* by Walter Brodie; *The Story of Pitcairn Island,* by Rosalind Young; *Descendants of the Bounty Mutineers,* by Harry Shapira; *Captain Bligh's Second Voyage to the South Seas,* by I. Lee; *Sea Life in Nelson's Time,* by John Masefield; *Life of a Sea Officer,* by Raigersfield; *New South Wales Historical Records; Pitcairn Island Register Book;* Memoir of Peter Heywood; *Adventures of Johnny Newcome,* by Mainwaring.

A NOTE ABOUT THE AUTHORS

Charles Nordhoff (1887–1947) was born in London of American parents. He spent most of his youth in the United States, and graduated from Harvard University in 1909. During World War I, Nordhoff served as an ambulance driver in France and later as a pilot.

James Norman Hall (1887–1951) was born in Colfax, Iowa, and graduated from Grinnell College in 1910. At the outbreak of World War I, Hall enlisted in the British Army. In 1918 his plane was shot down behind German lines, and he spent the last six months of the war in a prison camp.

Nordhoff and Hall met in 1916. The first book they wrote together, *History of the Lafayette Flying Corps*, was an account of an aviation unit in which both men served during the war.

After receiving an advance from *Harper's* in 1919 to write travel articles about the South Seas, they journeyed to Tahiti, where Nordhoff would settle for many years and where Hall remained for the rest of his life. Over the next quarter-century their literary collaboration yielded many highly successful novels, including *The Hurricane, The Dark River, Botany Bay, Men Without Country,* and, most notably, the *Bounty* trilogy — comprising *Mutiny on the Bounty, Men Against the Sea,* and *Pitcairn's Island* — which has been translated into dozens of languages, has sold millions of copies throughout the world, and is universally regarded as a classic work in the literature of the sea.

Look for these other exciting tales of nautical adventure

The Horatio Hornblower novels of C. S. Forester

Mr. Midshipman Hornblower

"English naval history comes truly alive. . . . The historical novel is rarely so well served." — *Times Literary Supplement*

Lieutenant Hornblower

"Sound history, absorbing adventure, and spanking good writing." — *Chicago Tribune*

Hornblower and the "Hotspur"

"In storm, in flame, in blood, and in love, the plot unfolds." — *Christian Science Monitor*

"No other contemporary writer can equal Forester at this kind of story-telling." — *Chicago Tribune*

Hornblower During the Crisis

"A first-rate swashbuckler." — *New York Times Book Review*

"Told with impeccable, salty craftsmanship and a fine, bracing conviction that history needs to be improved upon." — *Time*

Hornblower and the "Atropos"

"Delightful . . . everlastingly entertaining." — *Saturday Review*

"C. S. Forester's knowledge of the technical side of life during the Napoleonic Wars is a continual delight." — *Times Literary Supplement*

Beat to Quarters

"As gripping and realistic a sea tale as you are likely to run across." — *New York Times*

Ship of the Line

"A fine tale of the sea, to be ranked with the best of its kind."
— *New York Times*

"It contains such lucid explanations of naval maneuvers that before they have finished its readers may feel they could sail a frigate themselves."
— *Time*

Flying Colours

"Mr. Forester has a born storyteller's capacity for boundless invention, so that no two battles in Hornblower's experience ever sound alike."
— *New York Times*

Commodore Hornblower

"The colors are vivid, the heroics stirring. . . . You come away with the notion that life in the British Navy was indeed like this, the hardship and foulness along with the glory."
— *New York Times*

Lord Hornblower

"Enthralling. . . . Hornblower manages to muster consummate skill, bravery, aplomb — and that extra something that makes him the one and only Horatio Hornblower."
— *New York Times*

Admiral Hornblower in the West Indies

"The breezes blow sometimes for romance, sometimes for suspense. . . . Hornblower remains a hero and a dazzling jewel in the British Crown."
— *The New Yorker*

Available in paperback wherever books are sold

CPSIA information can be obtained
at www.ICGtesting.com
Printed in the USA
LVHW042034051119
636418LV00009B/1303/P